THIS
CAN
NEVER
NOT BE
REAL

This Can Never Not Be Real is a fictional account of a right-wing terrorist attack, but does not shy away from describing the realities of that experience. This involves descriptions of violence and the aftermath of violence, including serious injury and death. Additional issues dealt with include suicide, some discussion of racial and faith based micro-aggressions and negative body image.

Support and information for survivors of terrorism can be found at: https://victimsofterrorism.campaign.gov.uk/

THIS CAN NEVER NOT BE REAL

SERA MILANO

ELECTRIC
MONKEY

First published in Great Britain 2020 by Electric Monkey,
part of Farshore

An imprint of HarperCollins*Publishers*
1 London Bridge Street
London SE1 9GF

www.farshore.co.uk

HarperCollins*Publishers*
1st Floor, Watermarque Building, Ringsend Road, Dublin 4, Ireland

Text copyright © 2021 Sera Milano

The moral rights of the author have been asserted

ISBN 978 0 7555 0033 8

Printed and bound in Great Britain by CPI Group

1

A CIP catalogue record for this title is available from the British Library

Typeset by Avon DataSet Ltd, Alcester, Warwickshire

For anyone learning how to survive.
Hold on.

'In a murderous time
the heart breaks and breaks
and lives by breaking.'

Stanley Kunitz, *The Testing Tree*

ONE

TESTIMONY OF JOSEPH (JOE) MEAD, 17

I was watching Ellie Kimber dance.

TESTIMONY OF VIOLET NKIRU CHIKEZIE, 16

We were watching Ellie Kimber dance. Her dress was almost too short to be called one, and glittered like a mermaid's tail in the light. Her skin shone too – legs so long it was hard to trace where they ended. My little brother's hand tugged at mine and I looked down to see him twisting about to the music the way she was. It made me smile. Beside us, my mother tutted. But she was watching, too.

TESTIMONY OF PEACHES BRITTEN, 16

Everyone was watching Ellie Kimber dance. Like the brightest streak of silver in a crowded sky. Even if you hated her, you couldn't take your eyes off her.

I was dancing. It's the best way to forget everything, you know? Eyes closed, head back. Letting it all go. I fell into the music, the way it swam backwards and forwards, in and out of focus as I turned my head. The bass was like a heartbeat, the kind you feel instead of hear. I was crowded against the barriers at the front, right by the speakers. Close enough to feel the vibration in the air.

I know: not a good idea. I'm supposed to care about protecting what hearing I've got – but even if neither of my ears worked I'd have been there for the way the music trembled the ground, pounding up through my feet, close to how it feels when I'm running but without the pain or the focus, or the guilt.

. . . .

JOE

It wasn't even good music. Every year at Ambereve Festival the set list is the same: a couple of local legends allowed to twang their pitchy guitars somewhere other than talent night at the Queen's Head for a change, and then – headlining – Eric Stone. Amberside's one claim to fame. Even if his fame fizzled out, like, twenty years ago?

PEACHES

My mum remembers Eric Stone when he was big. Big as the Beatles, but with a better haircut, she says. She threw her bra at him once. Now he lives up on millionaires' row above the town, looking down on the rest of us. I just know him as the beardy old guy who shouted at me when I messed up his mic check. Dick.

VIOLET

His music isn't something I'd listen to, but the way Ellie moved to it was beautiful. It made me almost jealous, even though I could never do that – dance like that in front of everyone. I wouldn't want to, and not only because my mother would have tutted herself hoarse if I tried. She picked my name from a children's book she was given when I was born, and it suits me too well sometimes: Shy Violet. I'm not one for dancing. I like the quieter edges, where I can watch without wondering who might be watching me. When Ellie dances it's like she doesn't care if the whole world's looking on. And why should she? There's only her in the whole world when she dances. Just her.

JOE

She moves like she's . . . I don't know. Less solid than the rest of us. Like she hasn't got bones weighing her down. It's the same quality that turns everyone's heads when she glides down the hall at school. I can never keep my eyes off her. No one can. And it's not just the whole 'model' thing, though I see how other girls stare at her like she's got a secret – like if they could just figure out what it was they might be able to copy it. They look at her like they'd like to climb into her skin and become her.

That's how I was watching her then. That close. Couldn't help myself.

Sam nudged me, hooking his finger under the ring pull of my can and laughing as he nicked it off me. 'Careful, or they'll pop out of your head.'

I didn't even look at him. 'What?'

'Your eyes, mate.' He laughed again, but I knew he was watching, too. We all were. She was just –

VIOLET

Beautiful.

PEACHES

What a bitch.

ELLIE

I was waiting for the fireworks. Ambereve always runs
to the same pattern: there had been stalls down the high
street all day, fairground rides for the littlest kids, with staff
trying to keep cider-drunk students from hogging all the
carousel horses. Spiced apple handed out hot in little paper
cups – both adult and virgin varieties. Toffee apples.
Sweet cinder crunch twisted up inside striped bags. And
then the parade.

VIOLET

The whole of Amberside always comes out for the parade.
Especially this year.

ELLIE

It was cancelled last year, the parade, the festival, everything,
so this year felt like some kind of release, like we were all
taking one collective breath as we came together at the
start of the route. The numbers were probably the same as
they'd always been, but it *felt* more packed than ever.
Everyone wanted to be closer than before. People pressed
tight enough that it felt like we shared a single heartbeat
between us. It was beautiful.

PEACHES

They tell you to pick up a torch from outside the Guildhall and dip it in a beacon on your way past. For one day of the year no one cares that they're handing out sticks on fire to pissed-up teenagers, even if there's this one boy in my school who's famous for setting his own hair alight.

JOE

Dougie set himself on fire once. It was great. He was fine anyway, except for having no eyebrows until Christmas.

ELLIE

Then, like always, we headed up the road to Hearne House.

PEACHES

'Historic Hearne House' as they put it on the posters. We call it something simpler.

VIOLET

The house on the hill.

ELLIE

Everyone's either in the parade or watching it. Students from Clifton Academy and Sefton College, even the ones who'd say they're too old. Parents, pretending they're supervising. Little kids hanging off people's arms, asking for a turn with the torch.

I remember wondering what we must have looked like from above. All these pinpricks of light on the move, like shooting stars reflected in a dark, winding lake. Little comets. I'd found my parents' spot in the procession half by accident, and Mum was saying that there was something nice about a bonfire on a warm night, when you can still expose enough skin to enjoy it.

Dad glanced across at me and shook his head. 'Don't encourage her.'

I laughed, and lost track of them again as we crossed the bridge and I refound my crowd: Jessa, Cori, Sutton and a few others who were hanging on round the edges, hoping to keep up. The rush of people into the field felt like opening a door and letting a burst of heat into a chilly room. We ran towards the stage.

VIOLET

We queued at the bridge over the river. The house is a dot in the middle of acres of grounds, and the only way in is the bridge. Part of the river runs underneath it and then flows along the inside of the boundary wall, like an inverted moat. I did a school project on it years ago. To either side of the bridge the walls are built high and deep, turning the house into a fortress. It makes you wonder who they were trying to keep out.

PEACHES

Makes you wonder who they were trying to keep in.

I wasn't carrying a torch. I'd been at Hearne House since nine a.m., along with all the techies and other volunteers from the local theatre. The deal was that Amberside Dramatics were allowed to stage shows at the house three times a year, and in return we'd help crew for the other events they held there. Weddings and conferences mostly. Ambereve was the biggest event of all. We'd set metal lighting rigs up over a temporary stage, and were still running the last of our checks as the crowds arrived. Half the town had shown up en masse, forming a bottleneck at the bridge and finally squeezing through, one by one, to be guided by stewards to where they could throw their torches on to the Welcome Fire.

It's supposed to say something about unity, the fire, but I don't think many people stop to think how warm and fuzzy this act of mutual pyromania makes them feel.

JOE

The fire this year was massive. If there's one thing Amberside really goes all out for, it's arson. And the Welcome Fire wasn't even the main attraction. The field flooded with people waiting for the music and the lights. Dougie, Sam and me had to act fast to secure our usual spot on the southern slope, leaning our backs against the wall that separated the field from the private gardens.

When Sam passed my beer back to me the can was empty, but I wasn't really bothered. I was only pretending to drink it anyway. I'm an expert at faking it – you've got no idea the money I've blown on cigarettes I don't inhale. I was planning to get back into a proper workout schedule the next day, really do it this time, and since the month clicked over to October those early mornings start getting brutal even without a hangover. This year was already colder than usual. I wedged the can into the ground and kept watching Ellie dance, surrounded by the usual shifting crowd of girls desperate for her to notice them. We were waiting for the fireworks.

VIOLET

My mother said the display at the end of the concert was all she went for. Other people went to dance, to spend time with their friends. I went to spend time with mum. I'm not embarrassed. At home there's always so much to do:

schoolwork, taking care of Dad, a million errands. It always seemed a small miracle to have a moment to stand aside from everything and watch the dancing. And watch Mum waiting for the fireworks.

PEACHES

The fireworks are usually decent. They're more impressive than Eric Stone, anyway. But I didn't really give a shit about some pyrotechnic display, even if I had bagged myself a prime viewing spot. I hadn't wasted all day pleading for permission to spend the concert balancing on a narrow gantry above the stage for that.

It took me forever to convince the stage manager that he *needed* me on the lighting bridge, the chosen one who'd sit through the concert above it all, keeping one of our creaky follow-spots directly on Eric Stone's bald patch. He'd looked at me like I might make the whole rig bow in the middle. It didn't feel great. But it was worth it to see the whole world laid out at my feet once I was up there, so much smaller and less significant than it usually seemed. Even watching Ellie Kimber didn't feel bad with her so far below me. A complete reversal of our usual social status. Up there I could feel free of everything. Even myself.

JOE

'Taking their time,' Dougie was complaining, tipping his head back to look up at the sky. 'Don't they usually let them off during his big finale?'

Eric Stone was playing 'Rock Saw Us', which was his biggest hit and had got him the nickname Rocksaurus with anyone who'd sat through enough of his prehistoric, repetitive sets. 'Maybe he's got some new material,' I suggested. 'Maybe they're going to bring someone decent on to finish the show.'

'Maybe whoever's supposed to be in charge of them's been distracted by that arse,' Sam said. He pointed. 'Look at it.'

My focus was somewhere else.

Ellie Kimber was wearing a short dress with sequins that flickered every colour in the lights. It could have been sprayed on. I could probably have told you exactly how many strands of hair had come loose from the high, golden ponytail she was twirling round as she danced, but the doctors said I should expect to have some gaps in my memory.

I've got no idea whose arse Sam was trying to point out to me, either. That's not my mind playing tricks on me, though. I didn't even know back then.

I shot a blank look across at Dougie and Sam, I remember that. They were smiling.

'Come onnn,' Sam groaned, 'Join in.' And I had to,

didn't I? Dougie sprawled against Sam, laughing. Turning back to comb through the many bums being shaken in our direction, I pretended to find the one in question and give it marks out of ten.

VIOLET

The first explosion lit up the sky, and my mother's face. I watched her and kept the way she looked in my memory. She smiled so rarely that I stored away every one I caught. My little brother screamed and huddled in against me, and I let my hand rest in the tight curls of his hair to reassure him he was safe.

'Shh, Ade, it's loud but it can't hurt you. Look at the colours.' Still unsure, he wriggled until he could look up at me, and pressed his fingers to my face, telling me my skin had turned blue.

ELLIE

The sky cracked open in a shower of blue glitter. Blue sky at night, painting everyone beneath the same colour. One big explosion and a rattle of smaller cracks following it up. Better than the beat of the music. I tipped my head back to see what came next.

PEACHES

As the fireworks started, I hooked my legs and one arm through the rails of the gantry and let myself tip forward, feeling the centre of my not inconsiderable gravity pitch and shift. Two thousand faces looked up at me. Kind of a novelty when, at Clifton, I usually felt like the lowest of the low.

I think I must have been the first to see what was happening. I had that perfect vantage point. And I wasn't watching the fireworks, just the crowd flashing colours below me. I even slipped with my spotlight for a second, and let the rock dinosaur himself fall into darkness.

JOE

Sam caught a handful of the back of my shirt. 'What's that?'

VIOLET

'You're blue, too,' I told Ade, tracing my fingertip across his cheek as the lights shifted through a spectrum of electric colours, temporarily staining our skin. 'And now you're brown again. And orange. And brown. What colours am I?'

PEACHES

People had their arms in the air, eyes on the sky. They were swaying with the music, so it took a moment to register the other ripple of movement that started to pass through them. It was wrong somehow. Moving against the flow.

ELLIE

The world was noise and light.

JOE

Sam pulled me up by my shirt. He was on his knees behind me all of a sudden. He said, 'Joe, look.'

VIOLET

Ade grinned, reaching up to touch his fingertips to my chin. 'You're every colour, V.'

PEACHES

It was such a small thing at first. It was like watching a breeze skimming across a cornfield, snapping a few tall stalks in its wake. The crowd shifted beneath me, breaking away from the beat of the music, pressing closer together, confused.

Then something started to scythe a path right through.

TWO

PEACHES

People were falling. Twisting suddenly where they stood and tumbling to the ground. I couldn't understand what was happening. The fireworks were going off right above me. All I could hear were their echoes in my head, and all I could see was that, scattered through the crowd, people were falling. Not like dominos, chasing each other down. It was one here, another there. Random. I thought it must be some kind of joke. A flashmob. Something planned.

JOE

'What the hell?' I was getting to my feet by then, putting a hand out to Doug to pull him up because there was this girl staggering towards us doing that . . . you know that zombie walk cliché you see in bad horror movies? Arms out, reaching without knowing what they're reaching for? She was doing that.

VIOLET

There was a noise like a firecracker, except so loud it seemed as though it had exploded right by my ear. Ade clutched my hand – I'd told him the fireworks were too far away to be frightening.

JOE

She reached out towards us, me and Sam and Doug. And her chest was soaked, red-black.

ELLIE

There was a shove from behind me, hard enough to knock the breath out of my chest. It wasn't just one person. All at once, everyone surged forward. I was slammed against the barrier.

PEACHES

As everyone pushed away to one side or the other, all that was left to mark the path that had been carved through the crowd were the sprawled bodies of the ones who couldn't run any more. And at the end of the trail: two of them. Both in black, hooded, with scarves tied up over the lower part of their faces. They had huge guns in their hands: rifles or something. The kind you hardly think are real because you only see them in movies and games.

I couldn't tell you anything about them, not how old they were or the colour of their skin. From where I was they looked . . . tiny and world-changing all at once.

Turning, they picked a direction each and started firing again. Marking new paths.

VIOLET

Ade was squeezing my hand so tight.

Then he let go.

JOE

Doug reached her first. I was thinking – I know her. She's in the year below. Couldn't remember her name, though, and for some reason my mind was stuck on that. Her name. I know it now, from the photos, but . . . she looked so confused.

'Can we help? Can I –'

She fell forward into Doug's arms. Sam looked at me, his eyes all whites and terror. I was going for my phone. It's what you do when you've just seen someone die. Call for help.

ELLIE

People were climbing over the barriers, climbing over me to
get over them. In the panic I couldn't even begin to figure
out where the noise was coming from. Having only one
working ear is a recipe for distorted perspective – every
sound seems like it's coming from my right. Instinct more
than reason pushed me to move left, away from it. To see
if I could get over the barrier myself. I tried to reach for
Jessa's arm to bring her with me, but she shoved her
elbow into my shoulder, then a hand against the side
of my face, clasping my jaw in a clammy grip as she kicked
her way up and over. She didn't look down to see if
I was following.

Something hot spattered against the back of my neck.

PEACHES

A bullet grazed the metalwork of the gantry, setting off
sparks.

ELLIE

The fireworks were over, but there were still little explosions
going off around me. Lightless echoes, shaking the ground.
The barrier came down.

PEACHES

Everyone rushed at the stage in a tight pack that can only have made them easier to pick off. The band hid behind their instruments. I watched them crawl off to the sides. Stone spiralled to the ground in a dramatic twirl and dragged himself low across the floor.

ELLIE

It was like I was still dancing, except it wasn't me moving my limbs. I was being pushed one way then pulled in the other. A marionette without strings.

VIOLET

Ade was hit in the shoulder and the calf. I didn't know that then, though. Just that my brother's limbs had exploded in showers of blood and my mother was clawing at him, screaming his name as she dragged him up to her chest. He'd been too big to carry for a year or more but she pulled him up across her. Her screams were louder than gunfire.

JOE

It happened in a second, seemed like. That girl – Hannah, her name was Hannah – she fell and then everyone was screaming, the whole field was. Watching it felt like going insane. It didn't make more sense when I saw the first of them, a dark figure with a weapon in his hands, but it felt clearer somehow. I felt clear, and cold. There was someone shooting. A dead girl in Doug's arms. We were backed against a wall.

No one said anything. We ran.

VIOLET

There is only one way into Hearne House, and one way out. There were so many people scattering, running any direction they could, that they can't have known this the way I did. But my mother wouldn't run. She wouldn't even move. She froze there with Ade.

I wanted to do the same, but I knew there was only one way out of Hearne House and inside the grounds there were men with guns.

I slapped my mother. I think I'd heard once that pain could overcome fear but I'm still not sure how I knew it would work. I'm still not sure how I had the courage, even then, but it was as though it reminded her how to breathe. She looked at me and I told her how we had to get out. She carried Ade like he weighed nothing. We ran for the river.

PEACHES

I suppose I might've been safe if I'd just stayed right where I was, above it all. I'd probably tell anyone else: *stay there, you idiot, above it all. No one ever looks up.* But in the moment I felt more like a sitting duck.

ELLIE

Nothing would stay in focus. I couldn't see anyone I knew. The girls who'd been dancing beside me had vanished like a magician's trick. I felt under attack more from the crowd piling over me than anything else. Someone knocked me on to my knees. I got a foot in my face hard enough to leave a bruise. I was still trying to place the noise: where it was, *what* it was. Somewhere in me I must have known, but you don't think *gun*. You think fireworks. You wonder if someone's let off rockets in the crowd.

Something blocked my ability to accept the truth. Like my own mind was trying to protect me by pretending it just didn't know.

Then someone gripped my shoulders. One of the stewards, his high-vis vest flapping. I thought he was trying to help me up. Instead, he broke down my protective shell of denial.

'Why are they shooting at us?' His voice was a soggy rattle. He spat blood on to my face. I guess that when you're shot in the lung your body just tries to exhale it, like air.

21

PEACHES

The main thing was, once I got down, I wouldn't have to watch what was happening any more.

They'd stopped firing so indiscriminately by then. The crowd was thinning in places and packing tighter in others, and as I put one foot in front of the other to climb down the gantry ladder I could see their tactics change. They were choosing targets. Picking people off. Hunting.

JOE

I lost Doug somewhere, lost Sam somewhere. It was just *get out get out get out*. That was all that was in my mind.

PEACHES

I'll never know whether or not I was right, but I could have sworn I saw one of them look my way. I felt the back of my neck prickle.

VIOLET

Ade was crying. He was alive. It would be fine. We just had to run.

PEACHES

Then I was panicking. My hands were wet with sweat and slippy on the metal bars, and I knew I couldn't get down quick enough to dodge a bullet. I was still five feet off the ground when I let go of the ladder.

JOE

I want to remember it better. Like, I wish I could tell you about the bodies I climbed over, the ones whose arms and legs I had to step through like some messed-up playground game. I wish . . . I wish I could say I knew they were all dead already, that I couldn't have helped them somehow, but I can't. I don't know. I don't know if it was slow or it was quick for them, or how much it hurt.

It feels like somebody should know that. But I can tell my story. I can't tell theirs.

Maybe that's part of what I feel guilty about. They were just a blur under me, an obstacle. They were *people* but I just . . . I had to get to the river. I didn't stop.

PEACHES

My ankle took the brunt of the fall, at least for the couple of seconds it took to give way under me. I thought I had to have broken it, and if I had broken it I was going to have to run on it anyway. But I pulled myself up, and it held.

A look behind me told me either I'd been wrong or the shooter hadn't seen me. He was moving away.

ELLIE

The urge to run came by instinct, in a way it never does when I'm on the track. Everything in me told my body to move, but I was stuck. The steward had fallen on top of me and the people climbing on to the stage were starting to fall back, sniped and shattered like bottles on a wall. I pushed through limbs and got my hands wet with blood, and my stomach turned over and my heart was beating out of my chest but I had to get out.

VIOLET

People were jostling and shoving us, half of them trying to get to the river, and the same number trying to get away. It felt like being assaulted, but I kept my mother's hand in mine. We just needed to get out.

JOE

Get out get out get out in my mind, over and over, as if I didn't know any other words.

PEACHES

There was nowhere to run without putting myself out in the open. I knew there were two shooters, at least, and I could only see where one of them was.

ELLIE

I kicked my leg free – finally, finally I could move. I looked up. And he was coming towards me.

VIOLET

People ran past us, tried to run through us, slamming into the join of our hands. Pulling my mother away from me.

PEACHES

Climbing on to the stage wasn't an option. I'd seen what happened to the people who tried. So I climbed under it. I wasn't the first person to have the idea.

It was dark, which was something I was strangely grateful for, and quiet. With my eyes closed I'd never have known that the small alcove under the platform was packed beyond capacity. I could make people out by the paleness of their skin, the lightness of their eyes, but it was like we were melded together under there. I pushed myself into as small a space as I was capable of fitting.

I was on someone's legs. Soon someone else was lying half across my back. We were a haphazard pack of stacked cards.

ELLIE

I can't forget his eyes. Everything else about him was so inhuman: a bulky black outline with a sleek metal extension of one arm. But there was a strip of pale skin between his hood and the scarf over his mouth. He had blue eyes. They met mine. I tried to figure out who to pray to, if I should pray. There didn't seem a lot of point. I pictured my parents' faces and thought *I'm sorry* as loudly as I could.

PEACHES

I was looking into another pair of eyes, dark and frightened, belonging to a body stretched out along mine. Almost close enough to kiss. Slowly the darkness settled to let me see the outline of his face.

ELLIE

He turned away.

JOE

I ran straight into her.

ELLIE

I'll never understand why. He met my eyes, reloaded his gun, and walked away.

JOE

Straight, smack, full-on into her. Hard enough to knock her to the ground. But she wasn't a body, maybe just about alive or maybe dead like the others. I couldn't leave her on the ground and try to forget her. She'd tutored me through maths the whole of last term. She was quiet, always seemed unsure about something. I knew her name. I held out my hand and she clawed my arm to get back to her feet. 'Violet?'

VIOLET

It didn't matter if I hurt Joe. I wasn't thinking of that. I didn't see him even as I was screaming into his face.

JOE

I was gripping her hand, trying to say that we needed to get to the bridge. But she was just screaming, the words running into a high-pitched wail.

VIOLET

'I've lost my family. Oh, God, help me, I've lost my family.'

THREE

PEACHES

He was in my year. The boy the face belonged to. We had
the same form room and shared a couple of classes. I was
in the top set for English, like him. I had a feeling he was in
the top set for everything, the little shit.

Sorry – is it even legal to swear in front of an inquest?
Because I've got to warn you, it's likely to happen more than
once. This whole thing . . . it's the kind of experience you
can't really describe prettily.

Look, I know we're all here to help you understand
what happened that night. But I need you to know that
talking to us won't tell you *anything* about the people who
did this. You won't get the who and the why, or the
wherefore or whatever. And I'm glad about that, because I
don't care about them and what they wanted. I've seen
enough in the newspapers to last me a lifetime and I do not
care. I don't want you to care, either. Not about the men
with guns. But I want you to care about us, and the people
who were with us. The ones who were less lucky.

They're who matter. All I can tell you about the rest of
it is that there's no reason anyone could give me that would

29

justify what happened. Nothing that would make it forgivable. It was senseless, and if you're reasonable people, then you'll never understand it. *I'll* never understand it. And I was there.

There, crammed under the metal framework of a stage I helped put up the day before, staring into a set of brown eyes I *knew* were familiar. Genius boy. A rush of relief flooded through me just from recognising *something* in all the chaos.

In spite of that, it took several slow seconds ticking by before I could pin down his name. It wasn't the shock, or not totally, even if my own name could have easily escaped me right then. He was just one of those kids no one really sees. Unlike me, who'd kill to blend into the background as easily. When he'd joined the school he hadn't really spoken English. He'd learned, obviously, but by then no one remembered why they didn't speak to him – it was just his place to be overlooked. And he was kind of quiet and weird anyway, and too good at everything to ever get called out. That's why his name slipped my mind. But I got there.

He was called March.

JOE

'You can't look for them now,' I screamed at Violet, holding her hands just to stop her scratching my skin off. Every instinct I had was pushing me to drop her and get on towards the river, except one.

VIOLET

He was trying to protect me. It was the last thing I wanted.

JOE

'Listen, everything's gone mental. They're probably over the bridge already anyway. Get out, find them later.' It was never going to work: trying logic in a world that didn't have any any more. I didn't even know who her family were, but anyone with half a brain was trying to escape the same way we'd all come in. And the whole time we were stood there – it felt like an hour – we were getting passed by other people with the same idea we'd had: get to the river, get out. Other people's parents were shoving their kids in front of them, running, banging into us. I stumbled a few steps forward and dragged her with me.

VIOLET

It's blurred now, in my memory, but I know I was still fighting him until we were knocked apart. The same way I'd been knocked over and lost sight of my mother. People climbed over me, pushing me back as I tried to get up. My hands felt so empty.

JOE

She was gone in a second. I'm not proud, but I didn't go after her. My body just wanted to move. *I* wanted to move. Get out. I couldn't see through the trees, but I was close enough to hear splashes and guessed people must be throwing themselves into the river. The bridge would only let a few people across at a time.

VIOLET

One thing I remember too clearly is the way that people's screams change, between the time when they fear death is nearby and the moment it arrives.

JOE

The gunfire didn't come from behind us, but off to the right. Whip-cracks snapping through the air between us.

Like runners hitting the bend in a track, everyone forgot the escape route and veered left.

PEACHES

'You OK?' March crowded himself a little more into my space as someone twice his size wedged themselves up against my other side. It's probably the most ridiculous question anyone's ever asked me, or the most ridiculous moment to ask it, at least. But just then the normality of it felt like pure relief. We were safe. We were safe. Whatever the hell was going on outside, here we had to be safe.

'Pretty sure I'm losing circulation in my left leg, and whoever's crotch my foot's wedged in right now is unlikely to ever have children, but besides that . . .'

I let the whisper fade. Even I couldn't be British enough to say I was *fine*.

I think he almost smiled, though, before letting out a startled breath as he was pushed into me. A new body piled in over us, blocking out more of the light.

March turned his head as much as he could, looking through the net of limbs splayed around us. 'You'd think none of us had played Tetris before. We're definitely not making the best use of the space.'

'Tetris?' So he was quiet, and weird, and apparently into retro computer games and their application in moments of crisis.

Turning back to me, he raised an eyebrow. 'Sooner or later we're going to run out of room on the board.'

There was a half-repressed chorus of groans and hisses as another body fitted itself over the stack of others. I knew what he meant. Each new arrival could attract attention, and once this space was full, well, game over.

VIOLET

It was like going blind. I searched faces but couldn't register any of their finer features, just: wrong colour, wrong height, wrong gender. Wrong, wrong, wrong. Everything was blank to me.

Someone running towards me cried out and was swept to the ground like a leaf blown from a tree. I looked down at them, at the strange angles of their limbs. Wrong.

JOE

There wasn't any kind of orderly stampede, if that's even a thing. No one knew where to go. Some of them were still trying to make it towards the water, hoping to dodge the scattered shots – I watched as someone was brought down mid-dash, and ruled it out.

Directly ahead of me were the walls to the part of the garden that wasn't public, the part you had to book a tour to see. Entry was granted through an arched metal gate. People had battered it down already.

And I thought maybe there were ways out that weren't usually open to the public, too.

VIOLET

If there hadn't been a sudden surge of people to rush me along, I think that I would have stopped just there. I wanted to stop. I wanted someone to slap *me*.

JOE

So I smacked into someone, and it was her again. I don't know how it was her, in the middle of everyone else. Fate, maybe.

VIOLET

His face was blank like the others. Wrong.

JOE

This time I just wrapped an arm round her waist and kept on running.

VIOLET

No one lives in Hearne House any more, although there are two security guards on a rotating shift, and the curator has a small room in what used to be the servants' quarters. The lights inside are timed to turn on for a few hours every night, and turn off again without anyone touching a switch. But the walled areas are still called the Family Garden, and the flower beds are immaculate. The roses are prizewinning. There are heritage species thriving in the vegetable garden that have all but died out elsewhere. I wrote an essay on it once.

The blank world started coming back into focus when I first realised I felt guilty for trampling over all of that.

Isn't that stupid?

JOE

I don't know what I'd hoped for. Somewhere to hide, at least. Aren't old houses meant to have mazes or something? All the flower beds were worse than useless, just open black earth. I dragged her towards the pond.

VIOLET

The fish pond is populated with koi carp. It's hidden from the rest of the garden by decorative hedges in a pattern of arches and dips.

JOE

Other people were running onward, heading for the house, but I knew we didn't have time.

VIOLET

The shooting caught up with us. Five shots rang out across the garden. A man over by the pond, too far to help, started screaming, clutching his foot. Blood poured through his shoe.

JOE

I slammed her on to the path, just behind the hedge. Threw myself down over her.

VIOLET

Somehow I managed not to shout. There was no air left in my lungs, that might have been why.

JOE

'Why are they *shooting us*?' I hissed. I think I might have been crying by then. I can admit that. The reality of it was sinking in, now I'd stopped trying to outrun it. I was aware of every inch of my body, every centimetre of skin waiting for something to rip through it. I was pretty sure my feet were sticking out of the end of the hedge.

VIOLET

It was so loud. Not the popping of the bullets, but the echo that followed each shot, rattling around the walls like low-level thunder. The ground shook. There were cries, and worse sounds. Very close now.

'Because they want us to die,' I whispered back, too soft to be heard over the storm.

JOE

Then, silence.

VIOLET

Still not safe.

JOE

Either they'd moved on or they were reloading. I pressed my face into Violet's shoulder to keep myself quiet. My fear kept wanting to come out as a scream.

VIOLET

I could feel his breath against the curve of my neck. His face was wet.

I'd never been so intimate with a boy before, and it took

only a second to learn that there was nothing dangerous about it. It was only comfort. My hand splayed over his back, risking only the smallest movement. Words as quiet as breathing. 'We're OK.'

For that second we were.

JOE

The shooting started again, but you could hear it had changed direction. They'd moved on. I looked down at Violet, still not daring to do more than lift my head enough to press my forehead to hers and mouth it back to her, 'We're OK, we're OK, we're OK.'

PEACHES

The girl laying on top of me had started crying.

'Is she hurt?' March asked.

I did all I could to shrug, and snaked a hand out to find what I thought must be her wrist, squeezing lightly. 'Hey. Are you?'

There was some serious shoving going on from the other side of the space. Too many people were piled in for me to see what was happening, but I guessed our hiding place was reaching capacity and the people still trying to get in hadn't figured it out yet.

'Are you *hurt*?' I asked again. People weren't keeping

as quiet as they had been. There were murmurs rising all around us.

'My leg. And my boyfriend, my boyfriend –' When she cut off into sobs again I didn't ask her to go further. It was enough to make me grateful for the whole school career I'd spent single.

'What am I supposed to do?' I hissed at March, but I don't think he'd thought that far ahead, either. And then I couldn't see him any more for the knee colliding with my face, from a grown man scrambling over the top of us. I swore at him, trying to breathe under the crush.

He was the first of a rush. Everyone from the left side of the stage was suddenly pushing to make it to the right. The sound levels on the murmur turned up to a scream.

I saw black boots stamping round the outer edge of the stage, and then I knew why.

They bent down and started firing under the platform.

ELLIE

With the barrier bent and broken behind me, I watched the man whose blue eyes I'd met walk away. I watched him start to fire again. The bullets moved too fast to see but I watched them meet their targets. Watched people fall ahead of him.

I waited for him to turn around and shoot me.

I waited. Didn't run. Just stood there. My feet have

never let me down before but it was like my brain had forgotten how to reach them.

But he didn't. I'll never know the reason. He didn't turn, and other people died instead of me as he walked away.

When I finally couldn't watch any more, I crouched down inside the twisted wreck of the barrier and called my dad.

FOUR

ELLIE

The phone rang and rang until I wanted to smash it against something just so I could stop staring at the same screen.

PEACHES

She was hurt now. The girl with the leg and the boyfriend. While I was trying to keep my ribcage intact under the onslaught of people crawling and shoving their way over my back I could feel blood soaking through into my clothes. Hot and endless and not *mine* but I could be next. I felt sick. Sick and helpless. I was the sitting duck who'd crawled off its perch and smashed itself into a can of duck pâté.

ELLIE

No answer from Dad. Mum wasn't picking up. My friends were gone – I had no idea where. No one had stopped to look for me. 999 rang and rang and rang.

PEACHES

Of course, I was doing the same thing everyone else was doing, which was flailing around kicking and shoving and trying to claw my way out of a literal deathtrap.

ELLIE

Finally the emergency operator answered. I got the police, and a woman who didn't sound as calm as she wanted to be, telling me they were responding to the situation. *Are you somewhere safe?* the woman on the phone asked me. *Can you get somewhere safe?*

I think I must have started screaming.

PEACHES

March was the only still point in the flailing mass I was trapped in. I had to turn back to check he wasn't dead, and found him looking at me. Then past me, to where the edge of the platform was. The boots had moved on round the corner, sending another wave of bleeding, panicking people back our way.

He caught my elbow. 'Quick. Over here.'

ELLIE

Are you OK?

I texted Dad.

I texted Mum.

Tell me you're OK.

PEACHES

Maybe it was his Tetris skills that got us out of there. I don't know. He just seemed to be able to pick the right way through the gaps, even when they kept shifting and changing around us. Then he was shoving me out from under the stage, telling me to run.

I had hold of both his hands but he pulled back when I tugged on them. I frowned. 'What are you doing?'

ELLIE

I texted: *I'm safe. Don't come looking for me. DON'T COME LOOKING FOR ME.*

PEACHES

'Going to try to help some more,' he said.

And he just vanished back under there, like that was fine.

ELLIE

Love you.

PEACHES

Like it was fine that he'd probably crawled away to die when I'd just remembered his name and now had it stuck so hard in my head I knew I'd never get it out.

Like it was fine that everyone I knew could be dead. Everyone I cared about. I had no idea where the rest of the lighting crew were, even. Sally, Robin, Kirsty, Moz. I didn't know how to find them. Had no idea where they'd be.

None of it was fine.

But I ran, even without having anywhere to go. Before the black boots turned the corner again and I came face to face with something that had stepped out of a nightmare, I ran.

I didn't know how many of them there were: at least two.

Didn't know where they'd be.

All I could see as I looked up the field were people I hoped were just playing dead. People further up, running in every direction. The bonfire was the brightest thing there.

I made for that.

ELLIE

My parents always watched the fireworks from the back of the field, near the house and away from the crowds and the noise I loved. That had to be where they'd have headed when I broke away from them at the bridge. It had to be safer in the house.

PEACHES

Behind the fire, there were thick clusters of trees lining the river that ran inside the boundary wall. If I could get there, I could get to the bridge under their cover. That was the only way out that I knew of.

ELLIE

Pressed close to the wall, I made for the house.

PEACHES

I made for the river.

VIOLET

I had to find my mother and Ade. Joe kept me down until the echoing shots were rumbling too far away to be a threat, then tried to convince me to go to the bridge with him.

JOE

I still don't know how she wasn't just thinking of getting out.
Maybe I haven't got brothers, but Sam and Dougie were
close. Their faces kept flashing up in my head, but I knew
they'd get out. I just knew it. I had to get out, too. Then I'd
find them.

VIOLET

They couldn't be by the bridge, because I'd seen everyone
turned away from there by gunfire. If they hadn't turned
away, then I didn't want to consider what I would find.

I had to find them *alive*.

JOE

I couldn't fight her on it – I tried. And there was only so
long we'd have that bubble of quiet to make our choices.
I chose the bridge.

VIOLET

I chose the house. I knew the house. The lights were on, and
from across the dark field it looked like a haven. Inside, they
might be safe.

JOE

I thought about not letting her do it. I thought I might be able to get her out of there whether she wanted to go along with me or not. Who knows how that would have worked out.

'Stay safe,' I told her, and I let her go.

I went back the way we'd come. Back through the flower beds to the garden gate. Slow, because I was scared there'd be something on the other side of it, waiting for me. Slow, because this time I made myself look at the people who hadn't had my luck. Some of them were lying with upturned faces, some pressed into the dirt. They weren't all dead, but I didn't stop for them. What could I do?

There were fewer than I expected from lying there listening to the gunfire rattle off around me. Most of the bullets either hadn't found someone, or hadn't stopped them. Still.

Could I have helped? I keep asking people that. No one knows.

PEACHES

You don't know how terrible it's possible to feel until you're the one running for your life when someone who sort-of-saved you is left behind trying to save someone else. I like to think I'm generally a good person. That's my fallback, you know, when people give me the looks they do because of my

48

size, or how I dress, or anything. I'm a good person. I care. I'm not always nice to everyone, but that doesn't mean I don't want them to be happy and alive and not bleeding out under a stage.

Moz – he'd been one of the backstage crew at Amberside Dramatics, working tech with me for as long as I've been doing it. He knew me better than anyone – he always said he was going to get me a badge that read 'ask me about my great personality'.

I didn't feel like a great person just then.

JOE

It took a minute of cold sweating to make myself look out of the gate. I could picture the face looking back at me. The gun raised to my chest.

PEACHES

But feeling great wasn't really on the cards whatever happened. I made it to the bonfire. Still crackling.

JOE

No one there.

PEACHES

I felt more exposed than ever in front of it, with the way my silhouette must have been lit up like a shadow puppet. The shooting had stopped for now, which was good and bad because now I wasn't sure where anyone was. So I edged round the flames, and I don't know if I saw him or smelt him first.

JOE

But I could see people regrouping, going towards the river.

PEACHES

Sometimes I think I had to have imagined the smell. Whoever he was, he'd been too close to the fire. The shot he took must have knocked him back into it.

I think I vomited all the guilt and the questions out of me. When I could stand back up, I just ran.

JOE

I ran.

PEACHES

The bridge was a crush of people. Enough that you'd think it would have broken under them. I stopped for a second, just looking at it. Someone was *killing people* back there, and we had to queue?

And whoever thought inviting hundreds of people somewhere where the only exit is a rickety bridge was a good idea anyway?

No, I know that one. Nobody ever thinks something like this will happen.

JOE

When I saw the crowd shoving at each other round the bridge I slowed up, swearing under my breath. I considered my alternatives. The river that runs down Hearne Hill, within the walls of the house, is wide and deep, but if I could get down the steep, slippy banks without breaking anything, or just throw myself out far enough, I could probably swim it. Come back up from the other side and crawl along the inside of the wall to get out.

PEACHES

I'd almost got a spot on the bridge, I could *see* my way out, when the road on the other side of the wall lit up with the beam of car headlights. Now, I knew one thing from working on the concert set-up, and that's that cars don't go up the hill, unless they belong to the house. There's no proper road. You need permits and everything. But there was a car coming, and I could see people who'd made it out already running towards it. I had the same thought they probably did. It had to be help, right?

I read that five people were hit, there on the path. And that was before he got out.

JOE

I don't even know what went through my mind when the gunshots rang out on the other side of the water. On the other side of the *wall*. I heard screams go up from people who thought they'd made it out safe.

How many of them were there? It felt hopeless. If we couldn't get out, then . . .

PEACHES

You don't get used to chaos but at some point it starts to feel like the only thing you've ever known. I was running, I think, but I felt still. And I know I never saw the bullet, but in my mind I can rewind everything, play it back and watch it hit.

JOE

What was the point?

PEACHES

I can see it pass through my jumper. Feel the burn where it ran along my side. Just a graze. It was the shock more that the impact that made me fall, and that riverbank's practically a sheer drop. I fell all the way.

JOE

But the weird thing is, even while I was thinking that giving up would be the easiest option, my body wasn't going to do it. My mind just changed to a different track and the beat of *get out get out get out* switched to *just survive*.

I got down in the narrowest spot I could find between the trees to wait it out.

PEACHES

I can't swim. The result of a lifetime avoiding school swimming lessons has earned me a half-hearted doggy paddle and a vague idea that we can stay afloat *anyway* without all the humiliating kicking and flapping. So that was what I tried. If I could at least be still, maybe they'd ignore me. Maybe it'd seem like I was already dead.

Then the current caught me, and I found out that people don't just float.

JOE

When it had been quiet by the bridge long enough, I decided I could move further through the trees. I went on my hands and feet, as close to the ground as I could. I knew they'd be waiting, because people were going to keep trying to escape, weren't they? The ones who didn't know they weren't safe outside, either. I could hear the faint pop of someone firing right over on the other side of the field, five quick shots in a row, while the empty bridge sat there silently, like a lure.

Waiting where I was made it seem like a matter of time before one of the shooters got bored and started looking for shadows between the trees.

I kept my head down and followed the river.

PEACHES

I'd like to say I had some ironic thought about how, in the middle of a slaughterhouse, *this* was how I was going to die. But I didn't have any thoughts, except for how much water hurts when it gets into your lungs.

JOE

I was quiet, quiet, moving slowly and trying not to pay attention to the bodies that washed past me. There wasn't anything I could do for them.

Until one started spluttering.

FIVE

Control started passing reports through to us at just gone twenty-two hundred hours. 22:18 on the first call record I was handed. Having some paperwork to catch up on, I was in the station to hear the first details. A few confused calls, most of them cut short too soon to provide decent information. We started to piece together some talk about gunshots being heard up on the hill.

I wasn't too worried. It's the fireworks. We get reports like those every year. Ambereve's a local tradition going back years now, but some of the newer arrivals take time to get used to it. There's always somebody thinking things have got more dramatic than a small town should warrant. Especially these days.

Still. I had the desk try to get in touch with the officers we had up there. Only a handful. There was never much more than the odd teenage drunk and disorderly to be dealt with, and the house and organisers had staff of their own for basics like crowd control. We weren't getting any response, though, which was the first real note of warning.

I had them keep trying.

It was futile by then, of course. Taking our officers out was built into the planning of the operation. PC Danny Locke was shot first, we think, along with another volunteer working by the fireside. He was found there later. Time of death was not able to be established due to his condition.

PC Sally Ashford was shot at close range. We estimate this occurred just as the second shooter started moving through the crowd.

Many of the on-site staff were also sought out and dispatched at an early stage. These people knew who to target. There was never much of a chance.

With our radios silent and more calls coming in, I realised I'd made an underestimation. We had two cars on duty for the night. I sent them up the hill while I escalated the matter to divisionary level.

No one expects this from a small town.

It's never as quick as it should be to get people out of their beds.

* * * * * * * * * * *

SIX

VIOLET

'I'm looking for my mother. I'm looking for a Black woman and a little Black boy. Have you seen them?'

ELLIE

The field of hundreds had shrunk down to a scattered few. Everyone was trying to hide: pressing themselves into the hollows and edges of the walls, lying under and over each other on the field.

VIOLET

For once it had to be a benefit that there weren't that many people who looked like me in the town. Someone had to have seen them. 'Please, I'm looking for my family.'

ELLIE

She was different. Out in the open, approaching the few strangers who were breaking cover to get to the house as persistently as someone collecting charity money on a busy Saturday in town. She clutched for my hands as I got close and I almost pulled them away, afraid of her desperation.

We were all frightened, but my fear was a selfish, enclosed thing. She was letting it shine out of every pore.

Her hands shook.

VIOLET

My vision wasn't so blank now that I had a purpose, but she was the first person I'd truly recognised since Joe. How long was it since I'd been jealously watching her dance? I looked back across the field to the blacked-out arch of the stage as though she might still be there. As if that moment might be real, and this one just a nightmare.

ELLIE

She'd been asking everyone questions, but when I got there she just stared past me. I turned round to look, certain I'd see him coming for me and that this time he wouldn't turn away.

VIOLET

The stage was empty, but the field glittered.

ELLIE

There were little lights everywhere, blinking on and off and on again. People's phones lost in the panic, or still held in cold hands, going unanswered. On the other end there must have been hundreds of people calling over and over again, just wanting someone to pick up and say they were OK.

The news must have gotten out.

My phone was in my pocket, heavy and still. I tried not to think about why.

VIOLET

'I need to find my family.' I drew myself back from the memory of Ellie Kimber to look at the real girl in front of me. We'd been watching her dance. My mother's hand had been on my shoulder. My brother's blood was on my shirt. 'Ade, my little brother, he –'

ELLIE

Her mouth worked for a few seconds without any sound coming out of it.

VIOLET

'I think he's dying.'

ELLIE

She sucked a breath back in with a kind of desperate whining noise and let go of my hands to press her palms across her mouth.

VIOLET

Like I could push the words back in. What if saying them was the curse that made it true? But I had used those words and now I couldn't stop. 'There was so much blood.'

ELLIE

It was all over her. But it was all over me, too, cold and crusted thick across my arms. Someone else's blood, but not my brother's. I didn't know what that fear was like: I'd been too young when we lost mine.

I took her elbow. We were in the shadow of the house, but still too exposed. Not far away people were trying the heavy main doors – I'd seen boys ramming their shoulders against them in groups of two or three, but they wouldn't budge. They were probably bolted on the inside. The windows were high and separated into narrow rectangles, each crisscrossed with lead. Everything here seemed designed to keep us in or out, and the world had gone unsettlingly quiet.

'I'm looking for my parents too. I thought they might have got into the house, but there's no way.'

VIOLET

She didn't comfort me. I preferred that. But her hand round my arm gripped tight. It pulled me back.

I wiped the water from my face with hands that probably dirtied my skin more, but I didn't want to think about what was on them.

'No, there may be one.'

JOE

The girl's body rose up out of the water like a whale coming up for air. Yeah, yeah, I know it's not the most flattering description, I'm just – it's what I thought at the time. She coughed out some of the liquid from her lungs and I could see her arms pushing uselessly against the rock she was caught on before her strength gave out and she dipped under the surface.

A moment later she was struggling up again, coughing noisily, and I could see she was going to keep trying. And failing.

My first impulse wasn't even to help. It was to shut her up before the sound attracted attention. I looked back, trying to weigh up the distance I'd travelled in the dark. Were we far enough to be out of sight of the bridge?

PEACHES

Drowning hurts. I've heard some bullshit about how it's peaceful, euphoric even, once you run out of air. Well, maybe that's true, but the actual running-out part is just painful and slow. I'd gone from a hot, quick, crowded death to a freezing-cold, agonising one, and I was all alone.

JOE

She could have been shot, somewhere I couldn't see. There wasn't any point going in the water after her if I just turned her over to see half her chest shot away. And if she wasn't hurt, why wasn't she able to get away? I could watch her keep going under until she couldn't get up again, or risk joining her in there if I was seen from the opposite bank and picked off.

PEACHES

Eventually I stopped trying to breathe. It was as dark with my head out of the water as under it.

JOE

I didn't really make a decision until she stopped moving.

Then I was down the side of the bank before I could figure out how I'd got there. Somehow I made it through the mud-slips and the tangles of reeds without breaking my neck. I'd struggle to do that on a sunny day but I made it cold and half blind.

One leg in the water, I reached out far enough to grab her ankle. She was an inch away from being out of reach. Pulled her towards me. She floated. Everything was still except her red hair fanned out across the water.

I didn't turn her over. Just prayed she was intact as I hooked my arms under her and hauled her out and up through the river slime on to the land.

PEACHES

My memory cut out for a while, then in again with the sensation of someone punching me in the back.

JOE

I didn't know how you were supposed to get the water out of someone's lungs.

PEACHES

Not even mouth to mouth, can you believe it? Though given what I threw up – for the second time – all over the ground and myself, I don't feel too slighted by that. And I had bruises everywhere by then. What were a few more?

It was worth it to breathe in something that didn't taste like algae.

He didn't stop, though, even when I was coughing up half my internal organs.

JOE

I didn't stop until I heard her voice. Until then I didn't know if I was doing any good or just beating up a lifeless body until it shook.

PEACHES

'Stop *hitting me*. Oh my God.' I wasn't regulating my voice, but a second ago I'd been dead and keeping quiet wasn't really on my mind.

JOE

Out there it sounded like shouting. I panicked and put my hand over her mouth. Dragging both of us up the bank that way was a hundred times harder than getting myself down it. I felt every second.

PEACHES

I felt like I was getting kidnapped. Or mugged. In the circumstances, neither were the worst thing that could happen.

JOE

Maybe it's not something you're supposed to do to someone who wasn't breathing a minute ago. I didn't exactly have a manual. When we were back up by the trees I pulled my hand away, kneeling in to whisper by her ear, 'Keep quiet, for God's sake, there are people with guns.'

PEACHES

'*I KNOW.*' I whispered it as loudly as I dared, looking up to see who the hell it was that just fished me from the second of the night's certain deaths.

JOE

She got up on her knees, then twisted round and sank down with her back pressed against a tree. I could feel her staring at me. I was just fixed on her chest.

I mean, it was all there. No gaping holes.

PEACHES

So far as knights in shining armour go, Joe Mead was way out of my rescuing league. He's one of those flawless boys, where you don't understand how anyone can look the way he does without airbrushing.

I mean, it's like he was born with lash extensions, not to mention highlights and contour. He's basically beautiful.

JOE

And the rest of her? She looked like a swamp monster.

PEACHES

He can also be a basic dick.

JOE

Her hair was matted across her face, and her face was coated in green shit from the river and God knows what else. All of her was coated in it. She was soaked through.

PEACHES

All I really knew about Joe was that he hung round with
these two friends, also basics, and although it had been
a few years since any of them had called me names directly,
I could always feel the weight of possibility hanging in the
air when I walked by. Or hear the laughing when I'd
passed them.

JOE

And yeah, yeah, there was a lot of her to soak. Whatever. I
knew who she was, sort of. One of the drama crowd at
school.

PEACHES

Everyone knew who he was, though. If Ellie Kimber was
the school supermodel, Joe Mead was the boy most likely to
date her. I understood why there had been no mouth
to mouth.

    At least, for now, he looked as much like trash as I did.
Well, nearly.

JOE

She hadn't been shivering when I'd pulled her out of the
water, but it was starting to kick in now. My leg felt like I'd

put it on ice, and I'd only been in the water up to my knee. I could hear her teeth chatter. I hadn't realised how bitter it had got till then.

VIOLET

I'd never said one word to Ellie Kimber before then.

PEACHES

Joe Mead had never said one reasonable word to me in his life.

VIOLET

Now, I put my hand over hers on my arm and looked towards the house. That, at least, was something I knew. And I said, 'Come with me. There's another door.'

PEACHES

Now he was on his hands and knees beside me, pushing up close so he could keep his voice low as he whispered, 'You'd better take off your clothes.'

SEVEN

PEACHES

I spat whatever river water was still clinging to my lungs right out into his face. '*WHAT?*'

JOE

She didn't really get it at first.

PEACHES

With my chattering teeth gritted together to keep my voice from getting louder than the whispery, half-mouthed words he was using, I gestured down at myself. 'The last thing I remember there were people wandering around out there with guns. Which means we're stuck here waiting to see whether or not they find us. And you think it's a good idea to do that in the nude?'

JOE

'If the other option's freezing to death, maybe? Look at you.'

PEACHES

I didn't look at me. Looking at me is close to number one on the list of things I don't enjoy doing. I listened to me instead. The teeth I was trying hard to clamp together were clattering like a pair of tap shoes across a rickety floor. Drowning had been painful, but by the time Joe pulled me out of the water most of my limbs had gone numb with the cold. Now sensation was starting to creep back in little prickles across my skin, tiny electric shocks catching each other and pinching at my nerves. I'd been cold in the water, but I'd had other priorities.

Now I was freezing.

JOE

She looked less angry after a minute, like maybe she'd started to understand, but she didn't move except to look up at me with these wide, black-streaked eyes, and hug her arms round her middle. It was as though she was huddling in, trying to make herself smaller, but I didn't care about that. Her lips were turning blue.

'That's not gonna work.' I reached out to tug at one of the sodden sleeves of her jumper. 'It's like trying to warm up an ice cube while it's still in the freezer.'

PEACHES

He tugged at my wrist, and I unwrapped it a little from round myself. My sweater was heavy with water.

JOE

It was strange, sat there with her. Like everything else had switched off for a minute. Yeah, somewhere out there people were still dying. The world was still insane and impossible. But the circus I'd been part of had moved on for a while, and where we were it was quiet. It almost felt good to be worrying about something that wasn't just whether the next bullet would be the one that found me. For five minutes I got to put that cracking sound and the sight of people dropping out of my mind.

'Look, it's weird, I get it. It's not exactly the line I like to go in with, either.'

PEACHES

I wish I could say I hadn't wondered what lines he did like to go in with, but the big lie they tell you about waiting for death is that it's all you can think about. The truth is your mind takes any excuse to escape from focusing on the inevitable. I wondered about it, and I wondered if I'd ever heard his voice sound so soft.

JOE

She'd have to keep the thick-soled boots she was wearing, in case she needed to run. And the black culottes, they might be OK. But the jumper was swamping her in just about every way possible. 'But you'll dry off quicker without this.'

PEACHES

I looked at him for a long, silent moment. And I started to tug the wet sleeves down over my hands.

ELLIE

Violet tugged at my hands as I began to slow down. The windows of Hearne House were lit, a low gleam that made it through the curtains to spill out on to the path, and that just made the shadows between them seem darker. My mind kept telling me that it might be better to stay where we were, pressed to the wall, than risk running through the next yellow-bright pool of light.

VIOLET

I could picture myself standing in front of the house with my mother on an earlier, brighter day, filling a notebook with every single detail the tour guide was able to provide. I could reach back in my mind and retrace every word as though I was typing it into an essay.

The windows all feature transoms or stone mullions. The glass panes are run through with lines of black called leaded lights. The house itself is horseshoe-shaped, which meant the safety its shadows had to offer were deceptive. The house was full of corners, and we'd never know what waited around the next.

I gripped Ellie's arm and tugged her forward with me. We had to get round to the back while things were quiet.

ELLIE

The outside of the house seemed to go on forever. All high arches and jutting, squared-off windows with half-pulled curtains so thick you'd expect everything behind them to be tombed in dust.

People who'd given up when the door wouldn't give in clustered in the spaces between the windows or pressed themselves against stone pillars. Just waiting.

VIOLET

They say that George the Third stayed here while he was going mad. It was a hunting lodge, then.

ELLIE

Everything had gone so quiet. It was easy to think it might be over.

VIOLET

I don't know what they hunted.

ELLIE

We ran round the corner of the house and the gardens opened up ahead of us, vast in ways I'd never explored before. Skeletal arches of trelliswork ran like rib bones down a path towards a grassy amphitheatre, the green of the lawn washed to grey by the few scattered lights dug in between flower beds, so that visitors wouldn't break their necks in the dark. Ornamental bushes carved into strange curves looked like people crouching in plain sight.

VIOLET

Every so often someone broke what small cover they had and dashed for somewhere new. I could see the light of someone's phone being checked from where they lay under a bench.

ELLIE

And it sank in that my parents could be anywhere.

VIOLET

They could be anywhere.

ELLIE

If they were lucky, they'd have found somewhere to hide and stay safe. There had to be a hundred places in grounds this vast where the shooters wouldn't find them. But that meant I'd never find them, either, if I went running through the huge black gardens. I wouldn't know where to start.

VIOLET

If I imagined my brother hidden out there, under a bench, bleeding, then I imagined his death. He was so little, how much blood could there be in him?

　　I couldn't. I refused to think of that.

ELLIE

So we had to start with the house.

VIOLET

There would have been more to help him in the house. Ellie
looked at me, and I knew she must have been wondering
about the possibilities of those gardens. About whether going
inside would be walking into a trap. I thought that too, but I
knew the house. I knew my way around those walls. If death
came for us there, it might be easier to dodge.

She slid her fingers down to catch through mine.

ELLIE

Violet took us round to a fire exit at the side of the building.
I don't know how she knew the building so well, but she was
right: we would have been able to get in that way even if
people hadn't reached it before us, unlocking the metal bar
across and pushing it down and through.

The doors were hanging open when we got there, the
light inside orange and warm. An alarm panel on the left
wall of the hallway beyond flashed different alert-patterns in
red but there was no matching wail to announce an
emergency. I know it probably had some silent connection
to the security firm or local police – but where was the
police response I'd been promised anyway? I couldn't
understand it. By now there should have been alarms and
sirens, and safety on its way.

It was like we'd been left alone to die while the people
who were supposed to protect us considered their options.

I didn't want options, I wanted people with familiar uniforms walking us out in safe, neat lines and telling us not to look around. I wanted someone else to deal with this.

VIOLET

I was relieved and not relieved that the fire door was already open. There was a third door, a little further around the house. It led into the kitchen and was almost as solid as the entrance at the front. I had known this would be our best chance to get inside.

But I felt a new kind of fear suddenly, as though the doors being thrown back so wide could have been a trick just as much as they looked like an invitation. We'd never know what was waiting for us. But I wasn't alone. I kept my grip on Ellie's hand and went first.

ELLIE

Like they'd been waiting for us, a face appeared in the hallway.

VIOLET

A small, blonde woman with broken red glasses and a cardigan clutched tight round her waist. Miss Ewell.

ELLIE

She was our RE teacher at Clifton.

VIOLET

Even out of context she looked exactly the same as she did
when standing nervously in front of a class. She beckoned
us through, her hands flapping at the air, pale and quick.
'Elliot.' A beat as she looked at me, before she got my
name. 'Violet.'

There was the same relief for both of us in her voice.

'They haven't come . . . They haven't tried to get in here
yet.' Her words tripped over themselves but we both knew
she meant no one with a gun. 'It's safe for now. We're talking
about barricading the doors.'

Following the look that she threw over her shoulder,
I could see the small office behind her was busy. I recognised
a few in there as teachers. Others, parents.

ELLIE

Violet looked at me, and I let her hand go, then followed her
rush to the little cupboard of a room. It was too rammed
with people already, but I have the advantage of being
five-eleven in bare feet. Standing back, I could already
see that none of the room's occupants belonged to me.

Violet would have been able to tell the same thing for different reasons.

'A Black woman,' she was saying, using the simplest and most obvious descriptor. Amberside wasn't exactly the poster town for diversity. 'My mother, she has a green coat on, a dark jumper. My little brother's jacket is blue. He's bleeding so much, please –'

One of the women put her hand on Violet's shoulder and I watched her flinch away hard, as though comfort wasn't something she was ready for yet. 'Someone must have seen them.'

VIOLET

'Girls.' Miss Ewell spoke from behind us. She was trying to use the same voice she used to reassure and control a class, but it shook. 'Violet – I haven't seen your family, but they might have come through before I got here.'

I turned away from the room full of people who could pity but not help me. 'They could. I lost them just after the shooting started.'

ELLIE

'Why *are* they shooting?' I couldn't help break in. The question had hung in my mind since I'd been pinned like a puppet to the stage barriers. 'What's happening? Why are they doing this to us?'

VIOLET

Miss Ewell's face twisted as though the only explanation she had was tears.

ELLIE

'We don't know,' someone else's dad called over to us, holding a phone above his head. 'The police don't know. No one does.'

'Do you need a phone?' someone else's mum asked.

'I've been calling,' I said.

VIOLET

'I haven't.' The thought was an electric shock to me. My phone wasn't with me. Most of my calls were to my mother – it would have been a waste of minutes. But she would have a phone with her, just in case my father had one of his bad nights and needed her at home. 'I haven't tried to call.'

ELLIE

It was like something just lit up in her. I passed my phone into Violet's hands as Miss Ewell ushered us further down the corridor. 'We're telling everyone to go deeper inside. Find a room that you can lock, if you can.'

Behind us, two men were dragging chairs into the hallway. We'd just made it in before the barricade.

VIOLET

I led only because I was the first of the two of us along the hall. The phone was slippery in my grip. Entering my mother's number on to the screen I couldn't escape how much blood there was on my hands. My fingers were rough with it, but the screen still recognised my touch.

My mother's phone rang and rang.

And then picked up.

EIGHT

PEACHES

I slung my jumper down into a damp heap beside me. My shirt had peeled off along with it, the layers glued together like wet pastry. So here we were: me and Joe Mead, sitting under a tree, not even vaguely thinking about K.I.S.S.I.N.G.

I was thinking about my arms. Now I can't think of a more absurd thing to have been thinking about but, down to my culottes and a white vest top, my arms were the most exposed part of me. Too pale, and too big, I usually kept them hidden above the elbows.

That's how afraid I was of my own body. That's what had mattered most to me for so long, long enough that, waiting to see if I lived or died, I still had time to feel anxious about showing my arms. But you can't hide them, can you? Even wrapping them round each other draws attention. I was so *used* to worrying about that.

I looked at Joe, who was trying not to look back at me. 'So far I'm not any less cold.'

JOE

'You'll dry off faster. Trust me, I've watched a hundred programmes where men with crazy beards survive shipwrecks by jettisoning clothes and drinking piss.' I got to my knees, starting to unbutton my shirt.

PEACHES

I'd never watched anything about people drinking piss, and I had to admit I was uncertain about the appeal. 'If that's your next suggestion, let me give you a pre-emptive no.'

I'm not sure how audible my whispered words were through my chattery teeth. When he started undressing, though, I know things got clearer. 'Wait, what are you doing?'

JOE

It was cold, but I wasn't as cold as her. I pushed the shirt back over my shoulders. 'I have a T-shirt underneath.'

She started shaking her head like I was offering her the last can of food in a famine. 'I-I can't take that.'

PEACHES

It wasn't entirely that I thought he'd freeze without it. I also didn't think it would fit.

JOE

I held it out to her anyway. If she didn't put it on, I was
planning to just hold it in mid-air until she figured out there
was no point both of us going without. But I noticed
something when she unfolded her arms.

'You're hurt?'

PEACHES

The bullet that didn't kill me had taken a swipe along my
side instead. I couldn't feel it, still too numb with cold for my
body to start registering other kinds of pain.

I looked down. My top had a small rusty streak across
it that hadn't quite washed out and was torn a couple of
inches at my waist. I put my fingertips to it and found the
skin there slightly warmer.

JOE

When she pulled the rip in her top apart I could see it wasn't
deep. The graze wasn't even bleeding any more.

'Not much,' she said, and looked up at me. 'How many
inches away from being dead do you think that is?'

PEACHES

I walked my fingers slowly across my stomach, counting the steps until I might have been hit somewhere internal and important. There weren't many.

JOE

Then she took my shirt.

PEACHES

It fit. Just. I don't know how he'd been any kind of warm in it to begin with, but it made a small difference to me just to have one small stretch of my skin that didn't feel icy and wet. I was going to thank him when the ringing started. We both jumped like it was gunfire.

JOE

'Is that a phone?' Dumb question, but no one has a ringtone that just *rings* any more. Mine doesn't even have that as a basic setting.

'I think so.' Peaches was feeling around in the grass around her. It was too early in the year for leaves to pile up, but this seemed to be the only part of the garden they let grow wild. 'Here.'

PEACHES

Someone's mobile. They must have dropped it on their way through. I held it up for a second stupidly, then pushed it back on to its face again, covering the speaker with my hands. The light and noise were startling.

JOE

It was like a beacon, sirens wailing, flashing lights: *we're here, we're here*. I panicked and tried to grab it off her. 'Shut it down for fuck's sake.'

PEACHES

I didn't fight him for it. I've never heard a phone sound so loud before. 'What if someone's calling their family?'

He looked at me, a sharp, quick glare. 'What are we meant to tell them if they are?'

JOE

I picked up accidentally when I snatched it. For half a second I could hear a voice on the other end of the line – then I hung up. Showed Peaches the caller display before it vanished from the screen: *unknown*. If it had been family, the name would have been there.

Before they could call back, I dug my thumb into a button on the side and turned the whole thing off, dropping it back down, dead. But I was back on alert again. The bubble we'd been pretending we felt halfway safe in was burst.

PEACHES

The silence that flooded back around us had turned into something that could betray us at any second. I had to fight the knot that had clamped round my throat before I could manage a whisper. 'Someone could have heard that.'

JOE

It had sounded so loud to me I couldn't imagine they hadn't. The trees could have been hiding anyone. I nodded. 'We'll have to move.'

VIOLET

'Mummy?' The phone went dead in my hands. I dialled again, almost dropping it in my urgency. It had been picked up, just for a second. 'No. No. Mummy?'

ELLIE

From where I was I could hear it click to voicemail.
A woman's brief instruction to leave a message. Beep.
Nothing.

VIOLET

'She picked up,' I said, frantic. I tried the number again only
to get her pre-recorded answer. *I cannot get to the phone just
now.* 'She picked up, why won't she speak to me?'

ELLIE

I didn't know how to reassure her. Perhaps it hadn't been a
good idea for her mother to talk . . . but that thought wasn't
soothing. 'Do you want to text her? My parents aren't
picking up at all. It's what I tried.'

VIOLET

Another thought that wouldn't have come to me. I found
the app on her phone and fumbled through to create a
new message. What she'd sent to her own parents flashed
up first, unanswered.

ELLIE

She looked across at me. It felt like understanding passing
between us. I nodded. 'They'll reply when they can.'

VIOLET

Finding as few words as I could, I sent them along a thread
that I hoped would reach my mother on the other side.
*Mummy, it's Violet. We are in the house. Please find me if
you're here. Please call.*

I wanted to send a hundred like that, to just type
please over and over, like a prayer. Holy Jesus in your
mercy *please*.

ELLIE

She passed my phone back between two clasped hands.
I checked the screen for the Wi-Fi signal I knew wouldn't
exist this far above the town, then slid it back into my
pocket. I could call them again when we found somewhere
safe.

Violet was staring across the hallway as though she
could see a world beyond the wall. That half-second of
hoping might have done more harm than good, but I couldn't
have known it would work out that way. I looked at her
for a moment.

She's not someone I'd looked at often, if only because

– for the few lessons we had together – I could only see the back of her braided bunches from the front table she always picked. I knew her, though. Clever and prettier than she ever advertised: the girl who raised her hand with the right answer only after everyone else had given up. And she was on the peer-tutor team. I'd spotted her shy smile on their sign-up wall after I'd figured out that keeping up with my athletics would mean falling behind in lessons, and before I'd found out that no one cared.

I'd thought about asking to see her for help with my worst subjects, this year, but had hesitated over being tutored by someone technically in the year below, even if I was taking the same lessons. Maybe, when we were back at school, I'd finally take the plunge.

'So, you've been here before?' The question pulled her focus back to me, momentarily less haunted. I'd been to Hearne House before, too, but other than the concert every October not since a Year Seven school trip. She seemed to know it better. 'Because I don't know where to pick for hide-and-seek.'

VIOLET

She can't have known, but it made me feel less lost in my own mind to remember I was somewhere familiar. I had labelled blueprints of this house, building up my history project from the very foundations. I'd walked every hall. I had researched items of note in the gallery. But I didn't know which doors would lock.

It seemed unthinkable to go into one of the display rooms, where curators patrolled during the day to remind guests not to leave fingerprints on the tables or sit in armchairs that were stuffed two centuries ago. There were kitchens on the other side of the dining hall, but they'd be too large to be secured.

'Nor do I.' It would have been easier if I could have thought of it as just a game. 'We'll try upstairs.'

JOE

'Should we try the house?' Leaving the shelter of the trees seemed like a crazier thing to do the closer we got to trying it, though after the noise made by the phone it didn't feel safe any more, either. I still thought I could feel a target on my back.

PEACHES

We were staring up through a fussy, frustrating maze of an ornamental garden. I'd nixed going past the bonfire again, choking bile from my throat just thinking about it. I already knew what we'd find that way: the smell of burning and a pit full of bodies under the stage. I knew I'd want to see if March was one of them.

But I'd escaped that cage – I wasn't about to walk into another. 'Only if you like giant traps filled with musty antiques.'

He didn't look convinced. 'And you think the garden is better?'

I didn't think the garden was anything except not-the-house. 'I think it's bigger if we need to run.'

JOE

I could remember a bit too clearly what I'd seen happen to the people running while I was down behind a hedge. 'You're not faster than a speeding bullet.'

PEACHES

True. I had a long history of not being picked at games to prove that. 'But '

JOE

'And you can warm up in there. Other people will have made for the house, won't they? So, shelter, strength in numbers . . .' I'd started listing the pros off on my hand.

PEACHES

'Strength in numbers really worked out well when they were shooting their way through everyone in the field.'

It wasn't a fair way to shut him up and it wasn't really the same. In the field no one knew what was coming. Now we knew too well, and that was paralysing in its own way. Like us, stuck between the trees. But it was easier to be a bitch than try to explain everything I was afraid of.

Anyway, I knew we both had to be thinking the same thing.

JOE

It wasn't far to get back to the bridge.

PEACHES

Maybe the men and their guns were gone now. Maybe they'd been arrested, or moved on, or maybe it was all over and no one had found us to say so. Other people had been heading that way. We'd seen shadows moving slowly, one or two at a time rather than the rush from before. They were risking it. So could we.

JOE

The slow chant telling me to *get out* had barely started back up in my head before it was shaken out of it by the sound of fresh gunfire.

Couldn't tell where it came from. That's the problem with gunfire, unless you can see where the shooter is the sound reverbs back at you. Hearne House was surrounded by walls, amplifying it. It just sounded like it was everywhere.

PEACHES

It sounded so close.

JOE

We got down and started to crawl.

NINE

ELLIE

The first floor felt safer, putting one more measure of distance between us and what was waiting in the dark outside. And that new measure of security lasted for exactly as long as it took to hear the gunfire.

Once you learn that you're hunted, you learn to react like prey. Before, when the cracks and bangs could have been nothing more than someone setting off fireworks at the back of the field, I hadn't moved until the crowd moved me. Now my reaction sprang from some long-buried instinct that signalled my limbs to move before my mind processed why.

My instincts brought Violet with them.

VIOLET

Ellie pushed at the first door we came to and found it locked. We huddled in the alcove of the doorway instead and listened to the windows rattle in response to the vibrations of each shot. Her arms were around me.

ELLIE

Everything about me is built long. And I'm grateful for my body, when my long legs can carry me along the running track a quarter-second faster than the nearest competition, or my arms pull me an extra inch through open water. But sometimes I'd like to be the small one, the one capable of being surrounded. I've been taller than my own dad since I was fourteen.

I pulled Violet in, my arms round her shoulders, and tucked my head down, as close and as small as I could.

VIOLET

I've never hugged anyone but Ade so closely. It never felt natural until then. I could hear my breathing, my lungs struggling to keep up with my own panic, and the quick echo of Ellie's rushing breaths in the same space. That is, I think, what made me listen so closely. And then I understood.

'It's outside. They're not in here with us, the gunfire is coming from outside.'

ELLIE

I whispered into the space between us. 'Are you sure?'

Violet paused, holding a breath while she listened, then letting it out as a sigh. 'Yes. It echoes.'

VIOLET

It may not even have been as close as it sounded, but it was somewhere nearby. It meant that this nightmare was still going on. Each shot was one bullet's less hope, perhaps for someone that we loved.

Still, it was not in there with us.

ELLIE

I'd never wanted to be small and in my parents' arms so much. I closed my eyes and listened to the next round of shots tail off. Outside. Violet was right, once I listened the right way I could tell that the bangs came from somewhere else – even if not exactly where. It was the sound snapping back off the walls of the house that made it seem so near.

I was so glad to be inside. And so scared about who was still left out there.

Behind the locked door I'd pasted myself to, I could hear other people's panic, and others trying to hush the sound. I could've sworn I recognised at least one voice. I tried the door again, dragging at the handle. 'Sutton? Cori?'

VIOLET

Pulling at the door only raised another round of screaming from behind it. No one was going to let us in.

I touched my hand to her wrist.

ELLIE

She touched me, and pulled back, as though she needed permission.

VIOLET

'They've just heard shooting. They won't open the door now.'

Would we have, for them? I've thought about it since and I know that if I was in there with my mother, no, I would not open the door. With my brother? I would not open the door, no matter if there was a girl crying behind it. If I was in that room with Ellie, and we didn't know what was on the other side, I do not think I would open that door. But I believe that she would.

This was the first room, in the first corridor, at the top of the first set of stairs we'd climbed. The people inside were those who had been too afraid to find a better hiding place. 'There will be rooms that aren't locked. Someone will let us in.'

ELLIE

It was her way of saying *get it together and come on* without making it into a demand. I've learned that about Violet: she doesn't tell anyone what to do, but quietly lets them know what decision would be smartest.

I looked down the hallways. There was one on either

side of us and they seemed to go on forever, interrupted by doorways and little alcoves holding plinths and pots.

'It looks like there are quite a few to try.'

And she actually smiled at me.

VIOLET

There are fifty-seven rooms. Twenty of them original, the rest additions in the last two centuries. Fourteen have either been modernised or split to create two where there was one.

So, yes, there were a few other rooms we could try.

I smiled. 'It's quite a big house.'

PEACHES

The house loomed over everything. Without even meaning to we'd run from the shooting straight towards the front door. There were a few lights on in rooms across the front of it, some of them switching off and then on again as the shots rang out, and stopped. There were obviously people inside. That didn't mean we had to join them.

JOE

We were practically on the path up to the main door before the gunfire stopped again. Low to the ground the whole way. I finally dropped to my knees beside some probably

prizewinning rose bush and put my head in my hands.
'Listen, we've got to go inside.'

PEACHES

Literally every impulse I had was saying the opposite. Even if
a small part of my mind was desperate to put walls between
me and anyone who might want to shoot me, the rest of it
knew that ending up shut in *with them* would be worse.

Joe stopped, and I crawled back towards him into the
cover provided by a few worthless thorny bushes.

I started crying. Remembering it now, I have no idea
how it had taken me so long to reach that point. 'There are
acres of grounds here. They can't *be* everywhere, there
aren't that many of them. The people who survive this are
going to be the ones hidden somewhere in these massive
stupid gardens, OK?'

JOE

I didn't know what I was supposed to do about her tears. It
just got me angry, all the not knowing. How to help her, me,
us, anything. There were so many things I didn't know, and I
was so *bloody* angry. 'And the people who die are gonna be
the ones whose hiding places they find. You want to stay out
here and be a moving target running between the bushes?
Fine, piss off then. I want a position to defend.'

PEACHES

It wasn't the worst thing I've had said to me in my life, but it smarted like a slap across the face. My reaction was just to cry more, as though once I'd started I couldn't stop until it had all been shaken out of me. I pressed my hands over my mouth to muffle my voice until I could control it. 'Defend with *what*? An antique armchair? This isn't you at home playing war games.'

JOE

'You don't know *anything* about my home.'

Nothing about my life, nothing about my dad. Nothing about the thought that kept trying to get me to listen to it: that I could die here still wondering if he was proud of me, and at least if they found I'd died fighting back . . .

She didn't have a clue.

The anger pushed me up to my feet. The shooters could have been anywhere, watching me, taking aim. I didn't care. I was walking up that path like I owned the house at the end of it.

And then I heard my name.

PEACHES

There was a small light under one of the benches Joe walked past. Someone's phone. When he turned and dashed over

102

there the shadows behind it formed into two people who'd
been using it as shelter. I watched, still trying to stop
my tears.

JOE

Sam's face was sickly green from the phone light as I got over
there, but Dougie looked worse. 'What happened?' I was on
my knees, a hand on Doug's shoulder stopping him from
trying to raise himself up to see me. *What happened?* What a
stupid thing to ask.

What I meant was, how did it happen to *him*. Why
would it happen to someone I know?

I'd been taking for granted that everyone except me
would be all right. Doug tried to move again. I bent my head
down over him, letting his rolling eyes find my face in the
dark. 'Jesus. You're OK. Doug, it's Joe. It's me.'

He rattled my name back at me in response.

Sam was talking in the background, his voice a quiet
constant. Took me a minute to realise he was talking to
someone on the phone. 'It's Joe, he found us. We'll look after
him now. Yeah, I promise. We'll get him somewhere. I
think . . . I think he's looking better.'

There wasn't a way to look worse. The, um . . .

So at the hospital, after, they said after that one of the
bullets went into his hip and exited at the base of his spine.
The other one hit his arm and went right through. And

maybe that's right but there was blood everywhere and it was thick and cold where it had spread out from his side. It looked like glue smeared over the grass. And over his shirt, over his hair – everywhere I touched – blood.

When I looked up at Sam, his hand against the phone was wrong. Missing, like, a third of what should have been there. So I didn't know whose blood was whose, just that there was so much and it's nothing like you'd think. Nothing like I'd ever seen.

PEACHES

Joe just sat down, there on the path, where anyone could have seen him.

JOE

It was like someone tipped a lorryload of cement over me. A lorryload of not knowing what the hell to do.

'I've got to go, though. The battery's critical and I haven't got mine – no, don't call back.' Sam was on the line with Dougie's stepmum. She's still got half the call recorded on her answerphone. 'If you could do me a favour, though, and call my dad?'

When he rang off, he went quiet. Finally muttered, 'Five percent battery left,' like that was what I cared about, and tucked the phone into a pocket.

He wasn't looking at me, but he stared down at Doug, whose mouth was making words he didn't have enough voice to sound out. 'We've got to get some help.' Sam's voice wasn't calm exactly, it was just . . . empty. 'He can't use his legs.'

PEACHES

He'd walked away from me, fine. But what the hell was he doing?

JOE

Sam ran through where Doug was hurt: his side, his arm. He didn't know about his spine but suspected it. I only knew how it worked in films, when someone's blown away with a shot through the chest if they're going to die, or else helpfully hit somewhere distant. Somewhere that can be tied off to keep them alive.

Sam's hand would be fine. But what are you meant to do with someone shot in the hip?

'Should we move him?' I knew you weren't supposed to, but that was advice for after you've crashed a car or fallen out of a tree. 'If we just stay out here then . . .' There wasn't any help to get. It felt like there was none coming, either. If we stayed there, we'd just be watching him bleed out until they came and sent us with him. 'Do we just press down on it?'

I wasn't going to be any help. Helpless. The whole thing, helpless.

I didn't even see Peaches until she was crouching down beside me.

PEACHES

What else was I going to do? There was one place where there might be adult help, maybe a first-aid room if we were lucky.

'You lift him and keep him steady. I'll press down on the wounds while we get him to the house.'

TEN

PEACHES

I thought about it this way: why would I have been pulled
out of icy water if I was just going to die somewhere else?
Why would I have managed to escape from under the stage?
Why would help have shown up for me exactly when I
needed it, twice over, if it was just going to be third time
unlucky for me?

JOE

Sam had Doug's knees hooked over one forearm, the other
wrapped under the small of his back. I held his shoulders,
propping his head against my chest.

PEACHES

I have a relationship with God that's pretty similar to the
relationship I have with friends I only speak to online. They
seem nice enough but I don't know for sure that they really
exist, or at least that the girl I trade Broadway musical
bootlegs with over Tumblr isn't secretly a forty-year-old ice

trucker with a grease-stained beard down to his knees. So, I don't know if I think that fate's really a thing? But right then I had to let myself believe in it. It was all I had left.

I couldn't have been saved twice just to die for no reason. So it was OK to walk into the open with Joe Mead and Sam Hollander, who'd never have looked in my direction except to laugh in it before.

JOE

Peaches was sideways between us. She'd taken off the shirt I gave her and had it wadded up against the base of Doug's spine. Her other palm pressed into his hip. I could see the blood welling up through the gaps between her fingers.

PEACHES

It was OK to help carry Douglas Clark into Hearne House, even though it felt like walking into a trap, because I couldn't die now. Fate had made me invincible and just by being there I'd protect all the others.

Or something. I talked a lot of bullshit to myself on that terrifying, slow walk around Hearne House. But it stopped me from dropping everything and running away.

JOE

I sort of wanted to tell her I was sorry.

PEACHES

Actually, the closest I got to that didn't have anything to do
with being afraid.

JOE

But none of us said anything.

PEACHES

It was when I saw a face I knew.

JOE

The front door was a dead end, at least without a battering
ram. They built old houses like bloody fortresses, which
would have made me feel better if I wasn't on the wrong side
of the wall. We followed a few stray shadows vanishing
round the side of the house, hoping there'd be something a
bit less imposing round the back. I tried to keep an eye on
Dougie without looking too closely at him. Every step we
took must have hurt him, but stopping wasn't an option.

PEACHES

'Moz?'

I'd last seen him thirty minutes before the concert kicked off. He'd climbed the rigging above the stage to check the light gels with me, and we'd watched the last of the torchlight parade clump together to cross the bridge. It looked like they'd set the river on fire.

The lights were fine, and he should have climbed right back down to get his headphones on and talk to the director, but if he had five minutes spare to mess around, Moz always took ten. I remember . . . he'd hooked his knees through one of the metal struts and held his arms out wide, tipping straight over backwards until I almost lost my own footing trying to hold on to him.

He wouldn't have fallen. He had an instinct for heights. That was the thing: he was like a mountain goat up there, he always knew he'd be safe. And it terrified me every time anyway. I'd hissed at him that the only person scheduled to die onstage tonight was Eric Stone. That wording. Really.

'Him?' Moz had lazily slung one of his arms back round a railing, finally looking less like he was about to swan-dive into the bass drum on the platform below. 'Nah, he can't die. He's been a fossil for years.'

I'd watched as he climbed back down, cutting everything as fine as usual. Knowing he'd smile and everything would be OK. There were ten minutes before we started the show. I think now I'd call that moment the beginning of the end.

JOE

There was someone sitting propped up against the side of one of the pillars round the path. Peaches called his name. Not loud, but he was close enough to hear.

PEACHES

'Moz!'

He was an eternal pain in my posterior and also probably my best friend. Now he was slumped in the world's worst hiding place, only out of sight if you happened to approach his pillar from the exact opposite side.

He heard me. I know he heard me. I saw him flinch.

JOE

She froze up and for a minute I thought she was going to drop everything and go over there.

PEACHES

I couldn't get to him. One of my hands was splayed in Doug's back, partly pressing in against the bloodflow but

111

also keeping him straight in Joe and Sam's arms. If I'd let go the shock could have killed him right there. And I couldn't. I couldn't.

JOE

The guy finally spoke up when we were too far past him to really hear.

PEACHES

I thought he said, 'They won't let you in.'

VIOLET

The door we finally stopped at looked no different to the rest, apart from the sign.

'In here?'

'Does it lock?'

I swung the door inward to check. 'There's no key. But we can lock the doors inside.'

Ellie seemed uncertain, and for a moment I questioned whether I was mistaken in my choice. But I couldn't imagine even a killer coming into a women's bathroom.

ELLIE

The toilets at school have a gap under the door about half a foot high, so when you're standing by the mirror all you can see is a line of regulation black shoes. But there's this thing I do sometimes, which is to lift my feet and push them against the cubicle door, out of sight.

I do it most on the days when I know people will be talking about me.

I was thinking about that when I followed Violet in. The doors might be flimsy, but that wouldn't matter to invisible girls.

VIOLET

As Ellie explained how to be invisible, I found myself almost smiling.

'What?' she asked.

'I'd never have thought it could take so much effort for someone to go unnoticed.'

ELLIE

'You have no idea.'

I don't feel like anything remarkable, and I never have. But that word has followed me all of my life. Elliot Kimber and her remarkable rise. The remarkable start to her athletic career. The remarkable modelling shots. I've had remarkable victories. A remarkable survival.

That makes two remarkable survivals, now. Though the meningitis that claimed half my hearing instead of my life only killed one other person. And I'm not supposed to feel guilty about that.

'Though being almost six feet and blonde might have something to do with making me hard to miss.'

VIOLET

Those two things, and the days when her face was on the front of the newspaper, of course. I added one more reason, the most obvious: 'And being so beautiful.'

ELLIE

That word follows me less. When my feet are resting against a cubicle door I'm more likely to hear: *she's not even pretty.*

'I'm not the only beautiful girl in the school.' I would have told her I was talking to someone far more beautiful than I've ever thought I was, but it isn't the kind of thing you can say. Not when you really mean it.

VIOLET

'There are only three other Black girls at school, and still half the teachers call me by any one of their names rather than my own. If I could teach you invisibility . . .'

Be small, but not only in height. Keep quiet unless spoken to. Have half of your mind outside the school and half on your work. Let most of your classmates be unsure of how to talk to you, in case you're different to them. Look different. Be different. There are many invisible people in school hallways.

Far fewer like Ellie Kimber.

'But then, I didn't know about the trick with your feet in the bathroom.'

ELLIE

Talking to Violet made the threat seem further off again. We were inside and safe, even if a small voice whispered *for now* whenever I dared think as much. And the toilet block didn't seem to be a bad choice. It was obviously a new purpose given to an old room, assuming the Tudors hadn't had soap dispensers and Tampax machines, and the walls and floor were thick, white-tiled surfaces. The lights were bright, and if I sat on the edge of the washbasin counter, I could turn my good ear to Violet and didn't have to worry about catching my blood-smeared reflection in the glass.

My phone buzzed in my pocket, ringing on silent, and I almost had a heart attack checking the screen.

Jennifer Kimber Calling.

I knew that Violet's heart must have rushed into her

throat the same way mine had so I shook my head at her.
'My aunt.'

VIOLET

I watched her take a breath, hold and release it, before
hanging the call up unanswered.

ELLIE

It probably looked heartless. If this had made the news by
now then of course people would be trying to get through.
She was probably desperate. I scrolled down to recent callers
and silently blocked her number.

'I can't face telling anyone I'm all right. She could have
heard from my parents or she could not have done and I'd
have to tell her I haven't heard anything either and I just . . .
can't do it.' My voice felt caught up and strangled, my throat
squeezing down on every word.

I dialled Mum's number again. Then Dad's. It rang and
rang and rang.

VIOLET

She looked so very alone in that moment. I told myself that I
should touch her – take her hand – but those things don't
come easily for me.

After her calls went without answer, she offered me her phone a second time. 'Is there anyone else you need to call?'

ELLIE

She hesitated.

VIOLET

There was one person I wanted to call so very much. But I thought of what my mother would say, how much a matter of pride it was to her that she never asked for help. I shook my head.

'My father is very unwell. It would upset him, and there would be nothing he could do. It would be best if he doesn't hear about this.'

ELLIE

'Until it's over,' I said.

Her reply was quick. 'Yes.'

I understood that. I thought – if the ending to this story wasn't happy, at least we wouldn't be the ones who had to tell it.

But here we are.

ELEVEN

ELLIE

Of course, just as I was putting it away, my phone rang again.

PEACHES

They'd blocked the door. There was *one* easy way into Historic Hearne House, an incongruously white-painted fire-exit door, and the bastards already inside had blocked it with a heavy wooden desk and God knows what else piled up behind. I may not have *wanted* to go into the house, but I was furious that they weren't going to let me.

JOE

'For God's *SAKE*,' Sam yelled at the door. We weren't the only people trying to take this route in, and a small cluster of freaked-out faces turned to stare at him. It wasn't like he was giving away a secret hiding place, though, was it? Wherever the shooters were, they weren't somehow missing the big fancy house in the middle of everything.

Some of them were talking about breaking in through

the windows, but they were narrow rectangles, several feet off the ground. Yeah, maybe I could try to fit through one and risk getting grated on the broken glass, but Doug would be screwed.

PEACHES

'We're dying out here. You're leaving people to die!' Sam was still trying to shout through the door. He'd have been slamming on it if his arms weren't full of Doug's ankles. Other people already were. A few of them came over to shut him up. There was nothing Joe or I could do. We couldn't reach him.

JOE

The people around Sam talked in angry whispers, just loud enough for me to hear them. Ed and James from the football team at school. A couple of others I didn't know.

It can't be blocked too far back.

If we can get someone over it.

Just shove hard enough and . . .

Can't have been up long, they let Ellie through.

Ellie?

Kimber. We saw her go this way.

Sam looked at me to check I'd heard. Obviously I had.

'Can you get an arm free?'

119

'If someone helps.'

It only took a minute's planning, even if all of us were wondering how many minutes we had left. James stepped in to take Doug's legs, as slow and careful as he could.

And Sam called his ex.

ELLIE

Sam Hollander wasn't a name I'd have expected on my caller ID. We were friends. Sort of.

JOE

When we started Year Seven he was always going on about how he used to date her. Took a term before we found out it was while they were both still in nappies.

ELLIE

I mean, friends from forever ago. He used to live next door, and he was sweet, and then he didn't and wasn't, so we didn't talk all that much any more.

JOE

Since then we've always called Ellie the ex.

ELLIE

But I knew he would have been in the field that night. He and his friends are always tipped to be the ones making everything kick off at Ambereve, and most of that reputation is down to one of them setting fire to their eyebrows a year or two ago.

Anyway, Sam. I've known him since I was three. His dad calls me EllsBells. I still get cards from his family on my birthday and send them at Christmas.

VIOLET

'It's just a friend,' she told me, so that the frantic pounding in my chest would settle back to a slower beat. Then she answered.

ELLIE

'Sam? Are you . . . ? Slow down. Yes, yes I'm inside.'

JOE

Sam looked at us. 'She said she'll come.'

PEACHES

And, because Ellie Kimber gets everything she asks for, it wasn't long before we started to see signs that the barrier was coming down.

VIOLET

The conversation took barely twenty seconds, it seemed. When the call cut off, Ellie clasped the phone to her chest and filled in the parts I hadn't been able to understand. All I'd heard was urgency.

'They've blocked off the fire door and some of my friends are stuck on the wrong side. I think one of them got hurt. They want – I'm going to go and see if there's a way to let them in.'

She gave barely a moment's thought to opening locked doors that I would have been afraid to touch.

I offered to go with her, though the thought of retracing our steps set something stubborn in me wanting to dig in its heels. If we moved on from this room, then I wanted to check all the others instead. I had not found my mother yet, and if clinging to stillness and safety were wasting time, then going backwards was worse. But I offered.

ELLIE

I didn't want her to come. Whatever was happening on the other side of that door downstairs, it could be worse by the time I reached it, and Sam already sounded desperate. My mind was running races with what he'd said. He was a terrible liar, but could that change with a gun pressed to his head? I didn't know what I might be letting in.

'I think it's better if one of us waits. Then the room can't fill up with people who'll push us out. I'll bring them back up here.'

VIOLET

That was her way of making clear that the one to stay would be me. It did make some sense to make the bathroom a meeting point. Here we had clean surfaces, if someone had a wound. And . . .' The supply cupboard may have a first-aid kit.'

It would have cloths and alcohol, at least, the gentle products necessary for cleaning what's old and delicate. That might be something. I went for the door. 'This one's locked.'

There may have been other keys inside it. Ellie was right: one of us would do better staying to keep our claim on this space.

ELLIE

'We can try and break it when I'm back.' I slid off the counter and set my phone down on it, leaving it for her.

'In case either of our parents call.'

It was a wrench, but I'd be coming back for it, and for Violet. Neither of us had to see this out alone.

VIOLET

I took that for the promise it was.

PEACHES

Of course all it would take was a magic word from Ellie. Just one *open sesame* from her and the doors magically parted. Of course Joe knew her. They were Clifton Academy's sun and moon. Joe Mead, who never seemed to care about or want anything, and Ellie Kimber who everyone gave everything to. Some people seem to sail through life, and both of them were born in boats.

Please understand that I'm recounting how things were then. Exactly how I felt that night, and as I watched them pull back the huge desk behind the door, that was it. I'm not ashamed that I was bitter. I had reasons. They even seemed like important ones then. You have to remember: there was a lot I didn't know.

And I still didn't want to go inside. So my feelings were

pretty mixed when the desk came down and I could see a tall, blonde girl waiting on the other side.

JOE

You can't imagine the relief when the desk came down and we could see Ellie.

PEACHES

People rushed the door. James, the rugby player Sam had borrowed to help support Doug, all but dropped him as he got out of there. Or, into there. 'We have to take it slowly,' I warned, watching the muscles in Joe's arms twitch.

JOE

Must be some kind of herd mentality. Everyone runs and that's all you want to do. Just run and hope you're not the gazelle that gets picked off. Peaches was right, though. We went in last, and we went slowly.

There weren't as many people on the other side as I'd expected.

ELLIE

Miss Ewell and most of the people who'd been in the security office were long gone, probably taking their own advice about finding somewhere further in. I'd rattled doors until I found enough people to help drag the barricade down, and a couple of them ran before they could see what was beyond it.

The others started to push the desk back into place the second everyone was through.

PEACHES

The door would be blocked off again in no time, and anyone who wasn't blessed with the friendship of Clifton's most popular princess would be left on the outside.

ELLIE

From his voice and muddled-up words on the phone I'd guessed Sam was the one who'd been hurt. He was, but it was hard to notice the damage to his hand in comparison to the bleeding boy he was carrying with Joe and another girl.

JOE

'We have to get Doug down somewhere flat,' I gritted out, looking around for the crowds of waiting adults I'd expected to find on the inside. Somehow my mind had put together something off an episode of a soap opera. Doctors just happening to be in the right place at the right time, white coats and med kits in their handbags. At least some teachers lending a guiding hand. Not this. Nothing but a few kids pushing chairs down a hall. 'Isn't there anyone here to help?'

ELLIE

All the blood had frozen me. I'd seen people bleeding back out in the field, and the rusty stains crusting most of our clothes and skin, but nothing like the deep, tarry pit that a bullet had carved out of Doug's hip. The girl with them – Peaches – her hand barely covered it.

PEACHES

Ellie was it, the whole welcome wagon. I looked back towards the door. 'Can we get him down?'

ELLIE

'There's . . . I think there's still a table at the foot of the stairs.' Everything had been rearranged or pulled forward to become part of the barricade, and I'd hardly known where things were to begin with, but I remembered slamming my hip against it as I ran down.

JOE

It wasn't much more than a start, but we got Doug on to the table. I wished we'd given him something to bite down on when he cried out at how it jarred him. I wished I'd got myself something to bite down on.

PEACHES

Behind us, they were hauling the desk back to block off the fire door again, and with it my only chance of leaving this rat trap. I listened to the sound of old wood splintering as it squealed along the floor. Then I ran.

TWELVE

JOE

Everything else froze for a moment. I watched her sprint back along the hall.

PEACHES

It was Indiana Jones and I was being chased by a boulder. Doug was alive. I'd helped with that. I'd done what I couldn't have forgiven myself for not doing.

JOE

'*PEACHES!*'

PEACHES

I was getting out.

My own name echoed after me as I threw myself round the side of the sliding desk.

I made it through, and the door sealed up behind me.

JOE

Sam was calling my name. I'd thundered halfway down the hallway after her without even realising it, but I was too late. Even if I got them to pull the desk back down again, they weren't going to keep it that way. People in here were too frightened to let me go chasing after some idiot girl who could have gone anywhere once she got out. She could really run.

I couldn't just stare at the door with my fists clenched uselessly, either, though that's what I had been doing. I turned back, my breath heaving like I'd just run a marathon instead of a few pointless steps.

ELLIE

I had no idea what could have made both of them take off like that. Sam took over what the girl had been doing – pressing a sodden ball of wadded-up shirt into the worst of Doug's injuries. He looked as clueless as me.

'Is she a friend of yours?'

Sam snorted, 'Peachy? Yeah, we hang out with all the fat kids from the year below, now.'

JOE

'Peaches.' I snapped it sharper than I'd meant to, but the anger from before hadn't gone away. It was just redirecting itself now. 'And we'd never have got Doug in here without her.'

The effort could still have been too late. I put my hand on Doug's shoulder and he didn't even twitch. His eyelids were flickering but I didn't know if that meant he was conscious or not. What are you supposed to do when a hundred worst-case scenarios all happen at once?

'I told her to piss off when we were outside. She was scared of coming in here. Probably why she ran.'

Probably why I felt so shit about it. I had to let it go.

A breath. 'We've got to get him some better help. Isn't there anywhere in here – a nurse's office or something?'

ELLIE

'It's not a school –' Sam started, but I held up a hand.

'We found a supply cupboard upstairs there might be something useful in, but the door's locked. I can show you if you think you can break it?'

JOE

How hard could it be? If I'd taken the time to look at how sturdy most of the doors in the place were then I might have made a different assessment.

'I'll go. We can find something to smash it if we have to.'

ELLIE

I started up the stairs, looking back a second later when I realised Joe wasn't following me. Sam had caught him by the wrist.

JOE

He bent his head in towards me, and his voice was so quiet I knew he didn't want Ellie to hear him sound scared. Even with everything that was happening, somehow that was still important to him. The worst part is, I understood.

Swallowing hard, he looked down at Doug. 'What if he's dying? What if he dies while I'm alone with him?'

He wasn't. He couldn't. Those are the lies we tell ourselves when the truth would make our brains shut down.

Screw embarrassment. I wrapped an arm round Sam's shoulders and rested my temple against his. 'He'll be OK. All we can do is not leave him alone.'

'He'll be OK,' Sam was whispering as I left him. 'He'll be OK.'

ELLIE

Joe caught up to me halfway up the first flight of stairs with an apologetic smile.

'He was just telling me not to try anything with his girl.'

I raised an eyebrow. 'Actually, neither of you are really

my type.' But I didn't stop heading upwards. I had to get
back to Violet.

VIOLET

It isn't good to be alone and scared. It was amazing to me
how just one other person's company had made me so much
less of both those things.

For a while I sat in the place that Ellie had picked on
the edge of a basin and held her phone in my lap, as if she
were still here and we were both inhabiting the same space.
The bathroom was cold and white and the cubicle doors
hung partway open on their hinges, a dark space behind each
door. It hadn't bothered me before but, alone, I imagined
things waiting there. I got up, closing each one in turn
without checking behind.

I paced the narrow strip of tile I was left with. There
were noises elsewhere in the house, or perhaps outside.
It was so hard to tell. Sometimes doors slammed. Voices
raised. I heard, distantly, two cracks that may have been
shots fired.

You hear more when you are on your own.

I wanted to sit down again. Not on the basin edge but
on the floor, tucked small into the corner under it. The
disapproving twitch of my mother's lips came into my mind
and I thought of what she would say about sitting on the
floor of a public bathroom. The germs, the dirt.

I sat down despite this.

Pulling my knees in against my chest I closed my eyes and tried to keep the picture of my mother there. How soft she was. Her smell of soap and oranges. How much it delighted me to catch her lips moving from disapproval to a smile.

I thought of how she'd gathered me into her lap and held me this way when I was small. The day I'd come home from primary school and cried because she wouldn't let me cut off all my hair. Another girl had told me that birds would build nests in it and everyone had laughed.

If I was quiet, I could hear her voice as it was then, the way it echoed with my face pressed against her collarbone. *Now you listen, Violet. All I want for you is to be happy. It is all I want, in this world and the next. And if I tell you no today, you may think 'Mummy is being unfair.' If I tell you to work harder in school or to put on your smart shoes, or to leave your beautiful hair on your head, you may think 'Mummy is unkind to me.' When I say no it may not make you happy today. But know that I am saying it thinking of your happiness tomorrow.*

The next day, she let me put my hair into braids.

Perhaps not every *no* my mother ever told me was for the best. But I knew she always believed that it was.

Two more bangs from outside the house broke the picture I was holding in my mind into pieces. I couldn't say that they were gunshots, the sound was different from the rapid popping sounds of before. This was just two. Separate and individual.

I wanted my mother and my little brother. Just to hold them again.

Pressing my hand into the tiled floor I raised myself to my knees. 'Merciful Jesus, protect us now and deliver us . . .'

JOE

Nobody warned me it was the girls' loos we were going to. Ellie pushed her way through the door and there was this girl on her knees, with her arms and face pressed to the ground. Nobody warned me about that, either.

VIOLET

'In your name, amen. Amen, amen.' I had heard the door but couldn't cut myself off in prayer.

ELLIE

For one second I thought . . .

I got down on the floor and curled my arms round her. She didn't shrug me off. 'Are you OK? Has someone called?'

With a last whispered *amen* she wrapped her arms round me, quick but warm. 'No. I'm sorry. I just found myself too afraid that no one would.'

VIOLET

In prayer I'm not alone. And I was not alone with Ellie. In different ways, to have both in my life are a blessing.

She'd brought a boy with her.

'Joe?'

JOE

'Bloody hell.' I'd forgotten she'd run this way when we split up before. Turned out I'd just walked a long way round to end up in the same place.

Wouldn't have found Doug if I hadn't, though. Or Peaches.

ELLIE

Like me, Joe was retaking maths in Violet's class. The greeting still wasn't what I'd have expected, but Violet was only surprised for a second before she nodded, carefully unwinding her arms from round my neck and picking herself off the floor.

'Something like that. I'm glad you're safe, Joe.'

JOE

Still, all that and just I'd circled back to her. A slow trickle of guilt ran through my veins. I shouldn't have left her.

'I don't know about safe. We heard something that might have been gunshots on the way down the hall. And my friend's really f– *messed* up downstairs. Ellie said there might be something to help in there?' I pointed to the cupboard door. It looked like it might contain more mops and spiders than anything useful, but it wasn't like we had a lot of options to try.

VIOLET

Holding my hand out, I helped Ellie back to her feet, turning my head to look back at the cupboard. Now someone else was here I felt stupid for the suggestion.

'I don't know for certain, or at all, but they must have medical supplies somewhere – this house is open to the public. If not here, we can search the modern wing.'

JOE

I'd gone to rattle the handle of the cupboard, glad not to have to look her in the eye. 'Don't know that we've got that much time.'

I dragged back on the handle. The thing wouldn't budge. 'Jesus, these doors are thick.'

I don't think Violet minded. The whole taking-that-name-in-vain thing, I mean. If she could get some help out of believing what she did, then great, but I couldn't

see any all-powerful being getting that prissy about his
name.

ELLIE

'Maybe if we look for something solid in one of the other
rooms – a paperweight or something . . .' I was thinking
more along the lines of one of the table clocks I remembered
from our school trip, but didn't want to distress Violet about
destroying antiques until I had to.

VIOLET

'Or a marble clock.' The house had a fine example not far
along this hallway, one of the heaviest things I'd ever held. It
would certainly win in a fight against a door.

Ellie looked at me, startled.

I blinked back. 'What?'

JOE

Sizing the door up, I stood away from it and shook my head.
'No. I mean, we could try chucking a clock at it as a last
resort, but I think it'll give if we all go in with enough force.'

I *wanted* to kick the thing in. It might finally give my
anger somewhere to go.

THIRTEEN

PEACHES

Fate had realigned itself. If the house had both Joe and Ellie
in it, then it didn't need my potential invincibility to keep it
safe. The sheer energy of the good luck that shone out of
every inch of their gleaming hair and flawless skin had to be
enough to power a force field.

So I could use my own possible protective powers
somewhere they were needed more. 'Moz!'

He hadn't moved, still slumped in a heap of black
backstage clothes and untameable ginger curls against a pillar
that couldn't possibly hide him. His eyes followed me as I ran
across to him, but he didn't even lift his head.

Defeat didn't sit well on the face of a boy who could
hang upside down in the sky and know he'd never fall. Moz
would have been the last person I'd have expected to give up
on anything, least of all life.

'Are you hurt?' I crouched down beside him, a little too
aware that the pillar that offered shitty protection for him
offered absolutely zero for me. 'What happened?'

He looked bad, but only in the same way that I looked

half drowned and petrified. We all looked wrecked but not quite sunk.

Blood spattered his face in a way I was getting used to seeing – hardly anyone had made it out of the first attack unstained. We were both still alive. He didn't look like Doug had, with the life fading out of him with every breath. He was just . . . faded differently. I tried patting him down, trying to find what he wasn't telling me. 'What *happened*?'

Nothing, until he flinched when I got to his leg. He lifted it, slightly, enough for me to see that it was torn through, but not how badly. There was no oil-slick pool of blood on the ground.

'Where did you go?' he said finally. His voice sounded scratchy, like an old recording of itself. 'We crawled over the stage, where did you go?'

'Under it.' I bit my lip, wishing for a moment that I'd found him first, followed him somehow, even while I knew how many people I'd seen picked off that stage, arms fluttering like birds falling out of the sky. 'It wasn't the best move, but I got out again. Tried the river, then came here.'

I paused, waited for him to fill the gap. Then, when he didn't: 'You?'

'F-followed Eric Stone.' He took a ragged breath and pressed his eyes shut, keeping something out. 'He was . . . screaming about getting his helicopter here. Everyone was following him. It seemed like he knew what to do.'

When does it ever seem like the rock dinosaur knows what to do? When did Moz ever *not* know? The answer kicked in before my mind could finish the question: when he was afraid. None of us had understood what was happening in those first few minutes. Doing the right thing wasn't a result of keen decision-making, just pure dumb luck.

'So I . . . grabbed Kirsty's hand, and we followed him.'

Kirsty, the most likeable blonde I knew. Tiny in every aspect, and doll-pretty, and too unbelievably kind to let anyone feel bad about either of those things. She was like summer in the form of a girl, and Moz had been in love with her for at least as long as I'd known him. It had turned out to be mutual last April, and now they had a seam at their hips it was impossible to snip apart.

'He got to his trailer,' Moz said, 'and locked the door.'

'He what?'

'There were dozens of us outside. His drummer, stage crew, banging to be let in. He locked it on us. That's when they came.'

There aren't the right kind of words to sum up my thoughts about Eric Stone, but I've spent a long time looking for them. If anything had come close, I'd have been screaming it over and over, then and now. All I've got is 'bastard'. That *bastard*.

Moz's voice was dying out to a whisper. He turned his head, as if he was seeing things behind closed eyes.

'I pulled . . . pulled Kirsty down with me. She had her hands in mine, tight, and I was lying over her so they'd get me first.'

Then I knew why he hadn't been speaking. I was making him relive this, and now that I could guess the ending I wanted him to stop. To protect both of us I wanted him to *stop*. 'Moz, it's OK –'

'No, it's not. It's not. I felt the bullet go past my ear. It whistled past me before it hit her, before . . .' His eyes were wet, tears sliding past closed lashes. 'Her hands went slack. I tried to hold on to them and she wasn't holding back, Peaches, and when I looked at her –'

That was where the words stopped. The noise he made while he cried was worse, I think.

Kirsty Lansdown died from a shot to the head that sheered through hair and skin and bone and blew her scalp open. She was so to-the-core beautiful, I wish you could have known her. I'm glad I did. I cannot ever imagine how Moz survived her being taken away from him even while he held on so tight.

But he did. He held on, and he survived, and when the gunmen moved on there were only three or four of them who stood up out of the pile at the door of the trailer.

The trailer itself was riddled with holes too, of course. Being a bastard wasn't much protection in the end. But the press have covered that. No one's talked enough about Moz and Kirsty.

Moz had left the girl he loved, and half of himself behind with her. He'd walked along the walls of the garden with his fingertips tracing the brickwork, until they led him to the house.

And he found they'd locked the door on him there, too.

Now I'd found him, and I wasn't leaving him alone again. He'd curled into me, finally, crying against the thin straps of a vest that had only just started to dry off. I knew hiding in the bushes wasn't going to cut it. He'd been shot in the leg. I couldn't drag him on a hunt round the garden where the prize was hopefully getting overlooked by the people trying to hunt us down.

And I was sure hunting was what they were doing, by then.

I was trying to work out how to get back in the house with a phone that was taking a swim in the river and no flawless friends on speed dial to come and work miracles in opening the barricaded door for me.

But then two shots rang out, far too close for comfort, with space enough between them to sound targeted and deliberate.

And someone else who'd found themselves shut out in the cold with their worst nightmares made real arrived at the same decision I did, but took action first. I don't know who it was, but I looked up in time to catch the outline of their shadow.

They threw a rock. A heavy flat one carried up from the border of the ornamental pool.

And one of the ancient, leaded windows of Hearne House shattered in a shower of glass.

FOURTEEN

JOE

No first-aid kit, but Ellie ripped open a clean pack of cloths, and there were sheets, plastic wrap and a bottle of ninety-nine percent alcohol that I thought about just necking to take the edge off things . . .

It was stuff we could use, and Violet thought there might have been more in the rooms further along the wing. She was like a Hearne House human Wikipedia or something. But the bathroom was a start. The smooth, white surface the basins were sunk into looked like a good place to lay Doug out flat.

We'd almost hit the top of the stairs going back to him when we heard the window break.

ELLIE

It came from downstairs, though it made me jump as though it had happened right beside me. I looked right. They looked left.

VIOLET

We all three froze on the same question. Who?

Someone was in the house who, a minute ago, had not been. Whether they were in need of help, or here to hurt us, they were with us now. And we could not know which they would be.

JOE

'Go back.' I turned round, seeing the girls already starting to stumble over ways to argue with me. 'Look, I'm not trying to sacrifice myself for you, but it makes sense. Go back. Find some stuff from the other rooms that we can use to block the door with if we have to. I'll grab Doug and Sam and we'll get to you.'

I didn't give a lot of thought to how we'd carry Doug between just two of us, navigating stairs without breaking whatever threads were still holding him together. We'd just do it. A rogue voice in my head was telling me I didn't even know if I'd find him alive, but the smashing glass had rattled most of that fear out of me and replaced it with new terrors.

VIOLET

Ellie looked like she might argue with him. I was listening to see if more gunshots would come from below us, but it was quiet other than the distant sounds of panicked feet fleeing down other hallways. 'I don't think the broken window was too close.'

We could all go for his friend. There might be time. There might.

ELLIE

Joe shook his head, frustrated. 'Then I'll have time, but we still might need to block the door in a hurry. Just do it, please.'

Leaving his argument in the air, he pounded down the top flight of the stairs. I watched Violet make the same twitch I did to follow him, then stop herself. I stopped myself, too. For a minute we both stood there, caught between two actions. Between knowing and not knowing what was happening beneath us.

I know that I was waiting to see someone clad in black march back up the stairs, to make up for somehow sparing me earlier. I could – I can – still picture how blue his eyes were. They had been the only part of his face I could see, but they hadn't looked afraid. They hadn't looked anything.

How can you kill dozens of people and not feel anything?

'Why do you think they're here?' I asked quietly.

VIOLET

Ellie was still staring down the stairs, though we knew Joe couldn't get back so quickly. 'Why Amberside?' she asked, though she didn't address the question to me. 'It's just – we're nothing. Things like this happen in Paris, or London. We don't even have a proper cinema. We're just a random town twenty minutes from the city. Why us?'

Things like this happen in other places. I knew why she thought that. I understood the 'things like this' that she meant, but the truth is that none of the pictures we see on the news are ever the same. There are no 'things like this'. Each time it is different. Each time is a new knife, a new scar.

'It's always random, even in the biggest city. There will always be people wondering why they went to that restaurant, or sent their children to that school, or took that train that day. And the answer will always be that there was no reason to expect tragedy there.'

This was different, and not different at all. I didn't know who had chosen to kill us, or what their reasons were. They wanted us to die. That is all the commonality 'these things' need.

I took Ellie's hand. 'You won't find the reasons in us. The reasons are in them. And their reasons are *unimportant*.'

What mattered was that we didn't agree to die.

We had to find something to block the door.

PEACHES

I'd only got Moz to go inside by threatening to stay out there with him. Other gunshots had followed the first two. Another paired set, then a single crack in the darkness, far nearer than the rest. I was desperate by the time Moz pushed himself up to come with me. His leg was almost worse than useless – put more than the slightest weight on it and he went straight down again. It must've taken a huge effort for him just to get himself to the house.

Getting him to lean his weight on my shoulders made progress a little quicker, though it felt like wading through treacle from my perspective. It gave other people time to crowd round the broken window ahead of us. They came out of cracks in the woodwork – or the brickwork if we're going to be literal – deciding that whatever hiding place they'd chosen wasn't good enough any more.

We always think inside must be better than out, don't we? It's even in the language.

Safe as houses.

JOE

Sam was waiting by the table at the bottom of the stairs.

I took the last few at a jump. 'Still breathing?'

'Just about.'

149

PEACHES

Three people dragged a bench up to the window between them, knocking out the line of stone that made the frame too narrow to get through and roughly battering down the worst of the jagged glass. We weren't far behind after they climbed through. I got Moz through first and listened to the cry as he landed hard on the other side.

More shots from behind me. Closer. Quicker. When I looked back through the gardens I could see the silhouettes of people breaking out of their hiding places and starting to run.

I threw myself after Moz.

JOE

We'd decided to try lifting with my arms under Doug's shoulders and Sam trying to keep the lower half of his body in line, hips to knees, when the sound of rapid gunfire that had seemed to be keeping a safe distance until now was suddenly loud and close.

PEACHES

Down the hallway, other windows gave under a hail of bullets. All we could hear was breaking glass and the duller sound of stray rounds impacting a wall. It wasn't the room we'd fallen into, but it wasn't far.

JOE

It was coming from the left wing of the house.

PEACHES

We weren't safe, but if we'd been on the other side of the wall we'd have been dead already. For a second I wondered if all I'd achieved was a delay of the inevitable. Then I got Moz on his feet and into a limping run.

JOE

We ran right.

Stupid, it was so stupid. I mean, why didn't we just go up? The stairs were right there. We didn't have time to talk about it, so why did our instincts send us running along the hall with no idea where we were going?

I suppose the stairs felt too slow, too exposed.

I suppose we just wanted to move.

I don't fucking know.

PEACHES

The door was thrown open already, leading out into a hall that looked like every other hall in the whole damned place. Moz and I had run the lighting desk for a Christmas panto there the year before. I had hazy memories of escaping out on to a rooftop to catch my breath during the cast party, but the most of what I could recall was limited to the embroidered tapestries of the ballroom and the same four walls.

It didn't matter. The shooting had come from the left. There was only one direction we could pick.

JOE

Doors were slamming ahead of us. Sam shouted and swore as he ran and I didn't care about the noise because it drowned out Doug screaming. I'd got him against my chest, half over my shoulder because it would have been impossible to move quickly carrying him how we'd planned.

Sam tried a door, swore and moved on to the next.

PEACHES

We got to the stairs, and I gave myself three seconds to pick between sitting duck and duck pâté. I knew there was an accessible rooftop but had no idea of the way there. Except one obvious part.

We went up.

JOE

The hall was going mad behind us – everyone running through the house left to right. Passing us, slamming through doors ahead.

PEACHES

Two flights of stairs were all we made before Moz gasped into my ear, 'I can't.'

JOE

'Wait!' Sam got to a door before it could close on us, sticking his whole shoulder through and shoving until the person pushing the other way gave up.

PEACHES

It was a matter of time. If we stopped, it had to only be a matter of time until they caught up with us. If we stopped, we were done for. I looked at Moz, his legs shaking, his shoulder slumping into mine.

'OK. Let's stop and find somewhere we can mount a defence.'

JOE

The room we fell into was small and half full already. All the big, grand rooms were in the older wing of the house. This was newer, the part of the building where they didn't bring the tours. Someone had been using it as an office.

We got in, and about five people shoved through behind us before they tried closing the door again. As soon as the latch clicked, I wanted to get back out. It was too small and the window was a high slit in the wall, nothing useful.

Dead end. My own mind echoed through me. *Dead end. Dead, dead, dead.*

The door broke open again and tipped in another handful of people. We were pressed against each other.

Doug's weight was getting too much. Sam got down and crawled under the desk, and I joined him. I pulled Doug with me. There wasn't a lot of point in being careful how I moved him any more, but I tried.

More people got in. Just a couple.

A few others sat down.

'There's a hundred rooms in this place,' Sam said.

'Must be.'

He nodded. 'We're not going to die today.'

I sat and breathed in other people's air. There were screams in another part of the house. The crack of gunfire in another part of the house.

Then closer.

People were crying as quietly as they could.

Sam pulled the phone out of his pocket. He'd left it on, and with the call to Ellie the five percent battery life had drained down to two. I watched him scroll until his mum's name came up on the display.

No one else tried to get into the room.

They just fired straight through the door.

FIFTEEN

VIOLET

'Did you hear sirens?' I stopped pushing the chair across the floor and listened again, but it was gone. Ellie shook her head at me.

'I'm not the go-to person for "did you hear" questions,' she said, half smiling, although the tight way she swallowed showed how much she disliked the uncertainty. I'd noticed her asking me to place sounds before now, but it didn't seem strange. In panic it's hard to trust your own senses.

She tapped her left ear, a brief, gentle movement. 'I'm deaf on this side – I got sick when I was little.'

ELLIE:

And my brother, he died of it. So I'm the lucky one.

I didn't say it. Couldn't. Not knowing how scared she was for her own brother, then. But it put the thought of him in my head.

And my hearing isn't something that bothers me, most of the time. I learned my own ways of navigating the world when I was small – learned to be pushy about where I wanted to sit in social situations so I wouldn't be isolated on the silent edges. I never minded asking people to speak more slowly or clearly when I needed to.

'It just means I don't always catch things, or I can't always tell where they're coming from.'

VIOLET

It wasn't a flaw, just another part of her. Said so simply that all I did was nod and go on.

'I thought I heard something, but I can't be sure, either.' Perhaps I was imagining it. We'd brought three chairs through for now. When Joe got back to us we could bring a table from the room across the hall.

ELLIE

'If I could get a signal, I'd be able to check the news. There must be *something* happening by now.' There should have been sirens. Helicopters, police in riot gear, all the things you see on shaky phone footage after attacks. The army should have marched in to save us.

'I could call the police again? Ask how long we're supposed to wait for their response.'

The only response we needed from them was help.

I closed my eyes to listen for a moment, though the general white noise of movement around the house was already a distraction. It was hard to train myself to listen beyond it. Though the gunfire came through sharp, and clear.

VIOLET

Ellie's eyes shot open. She looked at me. 'Was that close?'

And I wanted to lie. *It's only an echo. It's just a trick. A reflection of something far away.*

We heard shattering glass. It might as well have been beneath our feet.

I have no talent for lies.

'Very.'

ELLIE

I still couldn't completely place it, but the breaking glass could only be other windows caving in. Or, coupled with the air cracking with gunfire, being shot through.

Bolting to the door, I yanked it open.

VIOLET

My hands were round her arm before I could stop myself, a useless attempt to pull her back. 'What are you doing?'

She stepped into the hallway. I imagined bullets streaking towards us, but I followed. For now the stretch ahead of us, up to the corner that turned towards the stairs, was empty. I knew what she must be looking for.

'We can't go after him.' It broke my heart to say so. I could still feel the quick beat of Joe's pulse so close to mine, the way he'd argued with me that I should think of my safety first. Now I tried to do as he'd asked. To think of my safety, and Ellie's. 'They will come up. If something is happening downstairs, they'll come up.'

ELLIE

'I'm trying to decide if we should use the chairs.' My skin felt iced over, cold fear turning me to a marble image of myself. Frozen. But Violet snapped me out of it. Her hands were too warm, her voice too desperate to ignore.

I could hear the rising panic in my own words. 'Do we wait, or do we use the chairs?'

Stepping back into the bathroom, the door swung on its hinges behind me. The clean, white tiles looked flimsier than they had before there was something to be defended against. The chairs we'd brought to compensate for the lack of a lock on the door looked spindly and breakable. 'If we block the door, we can't open it again – we'll never know who's on the other side. I don't know. I just don't know if we should.'

VIOLET

She was shaking. A tremble that started in her outstretched hands and ran through her whole body. As I lifted my hands to meet hers, I found an echo in my own bones.

ELLIE

We decided to wait. We'd count the minutes it could realistically take Joe to get back to us carrying someone with him.

VIOLET

Every three minutes one of us would check the hallway.

ELLIE

When too much time had passed –

VIOLET

Or someone in black turned the corner –

ELLIE

Or Joe *made it back*, we'd do what we could to block the door. And we'd pray it would be enough.

VIOLET

I made the first check of the hall and confirmed it was empty,
then stepped back into a room that felt like it had been
caught in a small earthquake. The shooting was directly
beneath our feet. It was in the room below us.

ELLIE

The way you feel the beat of a song through your feet, the
way I'd felt the fireworks rumble through me, I felt this.
A tile on the wall cracked.

VIOLET

There was screaming. I don't remember if I screamed too. It
was below us. It felt so close. Ellie grabbed a chair. I caught
the door handle. There was a clatter of feet down the hall
outside.

'Don't!'

ELLIE

I screamed at her. It could have been anybody.

VIOLET

'It could be Joe!' I stuck just my head out. Three people raced past the door.

I didn't know them.

ELLIE

Violet stepped back in and I rammed the first chair up against the door. It wouldn't fit under the door handle. All the time I'd been planning to ram the handle closed and then back that up with the other chairs. With the table we didn't get. It was such a paper-thin plan. I watched as it tore apart.

VIOLET

'I can't die,' Ellie was saying, words rushing into and over each other. 'I can't do that to them. I can't die here.'

ELLIE

Violet says that's when I told her about Adam. I hadn't wanted to. The words ripped out of me.

I was three when I came down with meningitis. It hit me first but it hit my little brother harder. For weeks afterwards, while the hospital ran hearing checks on me and talked to them about my recovery, my parents were trying to recover from the death of their newborn son. They never really have.

Dad had always wanted a boy. It's why I was given his father's name, Elliott, just in case there was no one else to carry it on. And suddenly, because of me, because he caught it from me, there wasn't.

I didn't understand guilt until I was much older, but since then I've felt like I've been living two lives in one. I have to do enough to make up for everything he never got to try. That's why I was trying to balance it all. Making a career out of athletics because I had a gift for it, not a love of it. It was why I trained every day until I hated running and my hair was green from the pool. Why I did the photoshoots even if it meant spending my lunch break hiding in the loos from what people thought of them. I was taking every chance I was given in case it all ended tomorrow.

Suddenly my two lives had dwindled down to one and it felt like that end was here.

The chair wouldn't fit under the handle.

VIOLET

It was hopeless what she was trying to do. Banging the chair up against the door and rushing out words about blame and guilt and love and responsibility. I knew those words well, but there was no time.

'Let me try,' I told her.

I took the chair and tilted it, judging how it would fit.

The door slammed open before I could block it.

ELLIE

The boy in the doorway had olive skin, a mop of dark hair, and a black shirt. I didn't know him.

VIOLET

I knew him. He was in all the same lessons as me. It wasn't his real name, but people called him March.

'Run,' March said.

ELLIE

'Run, they're coming. You've got to run.'

And he was gone. I didn't look at Violet, but I felt her make the same split-second decision as me. I don't know why – perhaps just because he told us to and it was a small relief not to have to make every choice on our own. We ran after him.

VIOLET

He banged every door open down the rest of the hall and shouted though it – 'Run.'

SIXTEEN

PEACHES

'Just leave me here. You should get to the roof, see if you can fly. I'm going to end up in the ground anyway.'

'Getting shot doesn't give you an excuse to go weird and morbid on me.'

'I can't keep walking.'

'We're not going in there. It's a bathroom – or a windowless deathtrap.'

'I can't. I don't want to.'

'Come on, Moz. One more door.'

We made it three doors down from the bathroom before his knee gave out under him again, and he wouldn't let me drag him on further. Half the rooms along this hallway had signs of being occupied not long before – furniture moved around, windows wide open – the bathroom we'd glanced into had held three antique chairs, crowded together by the mirrors like pretty girls communal-peeing at a party.

Everyone with two fully functioning limbs had abandoned this floor when they heard the shooting. If I was remembering right, there was at least one more level above our heads, plus an attic floor, plus the roof. If they were like me, the instinct would be to get as high as they could.

Though maybe we were high enough. The windows up here were tall and wide with heavy velvet curtains either side. The one in the room we'd picked was wide open and showed a drop that was only jumpable if you had an interest in breaking your neck. With all my courage lumped up in my throat, I leant out far enough to check the situation on either side. Nothing useful. The only ways out of this room were the door and the drop.

ELLIE

We climbed a servants' staircase at the end of the wing. The way was narrow and steep, the three of us having to keep one step behind each other all the way.

I looked back at Violet. 'Where are we going?'

VIOLET

This part of the house wasn't somewhere I knew well. 'I don't know exactly,' I whispered. 'I don't know if *he* knows where we're going.'

At the front of our little line March kept on upwards.

PEACHES

Moz had stayed by the door, his hands braced over the back
of a chair he was using like one of those walkers they give
old people when their hips have gone. He was *right* by the
door. I turned away from the window and shook my head
when I saw him.

'If you're waiting to make a run for it, we can always go
on a little further now.'

He didn't look at me. 'I'm just waiting.'

'No, what you're just doing is freaking me out. Come
on, you can wait a little further inside.' I put my hands on his
shoulders, and for a moment just held on to him there. I
wanted him to be the Moz I knew, my easy, confident friend
who always knew he'd be safe. I'd have felt safe with him,
even if it was a lie.

This wasn't the same boy I'd known for years. He
wasn't the same Moz I'd known even an hour ago, and I
wasn't sure he'd ever be that person again. But for all the
times he'd been a safe place when it didn't feel like there
was anywhere else in my world that was, I owed him the
chance to try.

We walked across the room together. Slow progress.
I didn't even know what this room was supposed to be – it
was just like the others, purposeless and full of random
elderly furniture that should have fallen apart years ago but
was being kept together beyond its time. Preserved, the

way moths are when someone pins them to a board.

I sat Moz on a pink velvet thing – I think it's called a chaise, and I think that's code for 'sofa' – that ran between the window and the wall.

We could hear shooting downstairs. It was inside the house now. Sometimes rapidfire quick, and sometimes those deliberate-sounding single shots. Every one made me jump. Shock rattled through my nervous system. There were screams, then silence, then more shooting.

On the walls, pictures of dead people watched me listen to people dying.

ELLIE

March stopped at the top of the final flight of stone steps, and turned back to us, panting. Even I was out of breath.

'Right,' he said. 'So now we need a plan.'

VIOLET

'I thought you *had* a plan!' Ellie exclaimed.

'Running was step one.' March put his hands up innocently. 'To give myself time to work out step two.'

PEACHES

I was quickly learning that Joe Mead was a moron. There
was *nothing* in this place that could be used to 'mount
a defence'.

I'd done a stocktake: stone clock on the mantelpiece I
might be able to hit someone with, providing they were kind
enough to not shoot me and would kneel down while I did it.
Any number of portraits in gold-edged frames: only useful
if I was attacking someone in a bad comedy heist movie.
Tables I couldn't get the legs off. An inlaid trunk too heavy
to push against the door.

Hearne House had been some kind of hunting lodge
once, back when it was surrounded by forests instead of a
ring road. Maybe there was a room full of crossbows and
muskets somewhere, but the rest of the house had fallen into
a stately repose.

Maybe Moz was right. All we could do was wait. I put
the clock down on the floor in front of the door, so we'd
have an early-warning system if anybody tried to open it,
then went to sit down next to him.

'If it helps,' I told him, 'I'm still hoping none of this
is real.'

It didn't feel real yet. Because the situation was insane,
and because everything I'd done had been while I was
running on automatic. Sitting with Joe by the river trying not
to freeze, or holding Doug's insides together while I could

feel his blood pulse against my hand already felt like a weird nightmare I was working on waking up from. Or just too unimaginable to be true.

Moz's hazel eyes were muddy and flat.

I swallowed as he looked at me. 'I'm sorry,' I said.

It was real for him. And hope wasn't something he understood any more.

He smoothed his hands across his knees. I wondered if he'd ever stop remembering how Kirsty's fingers had felt slotted into his. Or how it had felt when she let go.

'What I really hate,' he said, forming each word slowly, 'is that they get to choose. They could walk past this door. Open it and not shoot. Or . . .'

He ended the sentence with a breath, not a word. I exhaled too, feeling the air tremble as it left my lips. We both knew what the more likely choice would be.

'People don't get to choose how they die, so why should someone I don't even know be allowed to choose for me? We're *powerless*, we've got nothing, not even a choice. I've got nothing.'

My whole chest ached. 'You've got me,' I said.

His pale lips curved upwards, but it wasn't a smile I recognised on him. 'Yeah. Remember when we got up on the roof here, during that show? I told you I'd always wanted to fly.'

'You were drunk and standing on the edge of the wall. I thought I was going to have a heart attack.'

But Moz always, always knew he was safe. He wasn't afraid of anything.

He leant in and pressed a kiss into the river-slime tangle of my hair. 'I'm sorry.'

A single shot echoed down the hallway. We didn't have long before our choices would be made for us.

VIOLET

'The more scattered we are, the more of us are likely to survive. There are already fewer people on the higher floors, because most people hid in the first room we came to. They're picking us off one by one right now, but that's not effective.'

It was almost frightening how much March seemed to have figured out about the thought processes of men I didn't want to imagine having human thoughts at all.

Though he was right. Thinking of them as monsters only gave them power. If they were human, they were flawed, and flaws were a vulnerability.

ELLIE

'Do you think it's personal?' I asked. 'Are they after someone?'

'I counted at least three shooters in the field, maybe more, and there's someone else waiting over the bridge,' March said. 'That's a lot of people with a grudge.'

VIOLET

I didn't want to know their reason. I still don't. I know what's been reported, but I try not to listen. I won't read their manifesto. There is no reason, no motive, and no possible justification for what happened that night. If I do not know and do not care what their cause was, then I rob them of it.

They took so much from me. I want to rob them of something.

PEACHES

I ran to the wall and stood with my ear pressed to it. There was a long silence before the next shot came, and with it a corresponding painful thud of my heart.

'That wasn't the next room, but nearly,' I whispered. 'Moz, if you can go anywhere, we've got to go now.'

'I'm going,' he said.

His voice was so calm that it made me look across at him.

He was sitting with his knees hooked over the window ledge, his arms spread out wide, like wings. He held the edges of the frame, white-knuckled, and tipped his body back.

'Moz. Moz, don't. No, oh, please, don't.' My voice was loud. For that second I didn't care about the death outside the door, only the one in the room with me. '*Please.*'

He knew it gave me a heart attack watching him do

this, every time. Even though I knew he wasn't serious. He was never serious. He couldn't be serious.

I couldn't get there in time.

Moz chose. I watched him dive.

They told me he would have been gone on impact with the ground. Painless. Quick. Like he knew exactly the right way to fall.

He always knew he'd be safe.

The door thunked against the stone clock I'd set as a guardian, and I ducked into the only hiding place I could think of.

SEVENTEEN

It looked like a standard RTA – sorry, road traffic accident
– when we blued the cars up the hill. One vehicle, a blue
Astra, was skewed across the road, two casualties tossed
against the verge in front of it. The kind of thing you're more
likely to see on a busy road where people can really get up to
speed, get distracted on their phone, that kind of score.

But it happens on some of the country roads between
the towns, too. No room to pass, sharp bends.

The difference here was we'd passed crowds of people
running down the hill towards us. Some of them had stopped
and banged on the bonnet asking for help. We had to
prioritise. The ones able ask for it, they weren't the ones
who needed help most. So we carried on until we got close
to the car.

The other difference from a standard RTA was the man
with a hunting rifle stood to one side of the vehicle. He didn't
even turn to look at us, wasn't worried we were there at all.

He was shooting across the bridge, until he ran out of bullets and stopped to reload.

The other one, he had two more civilians over by the car. From the way both of them were standing I could guess he had a gun at their backs.

'Reverse, reverse!' I told the driver and yelled it over the radio, too. We don't carry arms, don't have that training. If they had hostages and weapons, then the last thing to do was panic them into killing even more. We were going to have to wait for specialists.

I radioed back to the station, not quite believing the words in my own mouth. We'd need counter-terrorism in for this.

* * * * * * * * * * *

EIGHTEEN

PEACHES

I counted the steps it took for him to get to me.

A long silence after the door had opened, scraping the clock along the floor. Then boots dealing out a heavy thud for the first three paces, before becoming softer, muffled by an antique rug.

Eleven steps to get to the window. Eleven steps of holding my breath so tight I thought my chest would burst. Holding in the tears that wanted to come. Holding in the urge to scream.

Though the narrowest slit of light I watched a black-gloved hand grasp the window frame. Watched him lean out. He smelt of gunmetal and the kind of overcompensating deodorant used for covering up worse things in every boy's bedroom. I could have choked. He was barely a breath away from me, but I wasn't breathing.

I could have pushed him. It wouldn't have taken much. A forward step, a shove. If I'd been braver.

I should have been braver.

I closed my eyes and waited for him to shove a hand through the thick velvet drapes that hugged in around me. I waited for him to spot that the curtains hung too far from the wall. Waited.

And counted the number of steps it took for him to turn round and leave the room without seeing me.

VIOLET

'Three of them for sure.' In a small, book-lined room near the top of the servants' staircase we tried to make the numbers add up in ways that might work in our favour. I counted gunmen off on my fingers, raising a fourth. 'And one more at least by the bridge. If he stays there, still three. This house has three wings, three staircases . . .'

ELLIE

'They'll have lookouts.' March used his fingertip to tap down the fourth of Violet's gunmen, hesitating over ruling out a second. 'When the police do get here, they don't want to be taken by surprise.'

'They only need one.' I waved his hand away. 'The bridge is the only way in.'

Violet nodded as I checked with her for confirmation. Even before we came inside Hearne House itself, we'd been bricked in with them.

Our calculations were close. Except that there were two men in the car at the bridge, using hostages to keep the police from shooting right through them. I know some people have asked whether it was worth the delay, trying to preserve two lives pressed against the bonnet of a terrorist's car, while the rest of us were being hunted down with no sign that help was even trying to reach us.

As someone counted among 'the rest of us', I can't wish that one person had died instead of another. Life isn't something you can trade based on what we're worth.

VIOLET

'Then if we assume all three are in here, there could be one on each side coming to meet in the middle.' This was the worst of possibilities, and it was what I would plan if I wanted to check every room. 'Or would they stay as a group and move across?'

One of them might be ambushed by enough of us. The shots we had heard so far hadn't been too widely scattered, and they were fewer and further between. If we were lucky, if perhaps there was only one of them, or three moving together – they might be easier to avoid.

'Would all three come in? There have to be more people outside the house than in it.' Ellie smoothed her hands over her hair. She'd done it so often as we talked that now she was only pulling more bright strands loose from her ponytail.

I looked at her, knowing we were both thinking of our

178

parents. I thought, *If my family are not in here, then give me all three gunmen. Let them spend their time hunting me.*

ELLIE

'There'll be more people outside, but harder to find,' March said. 'They could corner groups of us in here. Out in the gardens they were just chasing people running around in the dark.'

And the house was all lit up for them. It was half the reason I'd felt safe once we were in here, but of course the same beacon that drew us all in would have drawn them, too.

Getting nowhere was frustrating enough. Standing still while we got there was worse. My calf muscles were twitching. 'So we have no idea how many there are, or how they're likely to work, and coming in here for protection only made us easier to find. From what you're saying, where we hide doesn't even matter. We're just taking our pick in a lucky dip.'

VIOLET

'Not quite.' It wasn't Ellie's frustration, but something March had said that caught me. 'In here they're not chasing us around in the dark. But they could be.' I watched their faces.

'If we go around switching lights off, we can't not run

into them,' Ellie said. 'And they could turn them back on –'

'Not if we turn them all off at once.' March was smiling. He slapped me on the shoulder hard enough that I ducked and yelped.

'We can turn off the power to the house,' I said, rubbing a hand where my arm felt numb. 'I think I know where the mains switch must be.'

ELLIE

We'd have to get downstairs again. Achieving a modern electrical supply in an ancient building hadn't been part of any of Violet's studies about Hearne House, but she had been shown the cellars: a rocky archway where wine was still kept for the parties hosted there. She'd seen a doorway with a yellow exclamation mark, out of place in all the whitewashed stone. It would have to be through there.

Or it would have to be worth a try.

Though the idea of retracing our steps all the way back to the ground floor smoothed out all the twitches that had made my muscles want to move, and rooted my feet. We all stood silently, listening.

VIOLET

The shooting had stopped. We were starting to learn that any sense of security in that was false.

'Reloading?' I kept my voice to a whisper.

'Or there's no one left down there to find.' March kept his voice just as soft. It was as though we wouldn't hear a bullet over anything more than a murmur. 'When they're panicking, most people are going to shut themselves in the first room they come to. The higher up, the fewer of us.'

I thought of Joe.

ELLIE

I thought of Sam and Joe. Not just stuck on the crowded ground floor but weighed down by their best friend. I wondered if they'd abandoned Doug, or if the shooters might have passed over someone who already looked so finished.

I tried to count the gunshots we'd heard once we knew they were inside the house. Far, far too many. Enough for everyone I was afraid for.

'But they'll have moved on by now. We'll go down.'

VIOLET

The plan, as much as it was a plan and not simply a mutual agreement to hope luck would be on our side, was to move back down the narrow staircase one level, and then go through the centre of the house.

ELLIE

March reasoned that, even with three of them, the centre would be where they spent the least time. Either they'd come up that way and work their way outward, or come from the sides and work in.

The hallways would be the real danger. So we'd only cross one before we made it to the ground.

VIOLET

We were already almost at the highest point of the house. To the side of us were only the curator's private rooms and the attic. There were two floors between us and the ground level. First, we'd go back down the narrow staircase, knowing that if we met someone coming up, there would be nowhere to escape to but a bedroom and a small room lined with books.

'If we can be quiet enough, we'd hear anyone coming up before they heard us.' March tried to be reassuring, but he didn't move.

I went to the stairs first. Took off my shoes.

ELLIE

There must be an extra wire in the nervous system of people like Violet. A synaptic thread that flashes impulses of

182

brilliance along it, whether she's calculating the square route of pi or jumping to an obvious conclusion that no one else had reached: socked feet are quieter.

I stepped out of my shoes. March pulled off his boots. Violet led us back into the echoey staircase, this time minus any echoes of our own.

We were all listening. I was concentrating so hard on every ambient noise that I almost tripped.

VIOLET

At the first landing we stopped. It had been agreed that this would be where we'd cross to the central stairs. We'd heard no shots from so high up, so it was possible that our hunters had not reached this floor yet, or had given up on finding further prey.

One of us would go first, to see that the rooms were clear, and signal.

ELLIE

Violet protested against the idea of splitting up, even for the length of one hallway, but it had seemed right to me. If we had to run, one person could run alone more easily without keeping track of the others.

And if one of us had to run, it was going to be me.

I crept along one side of the hallway, body slowing by

every open doorway, heart racing until I found it empty. And then I came to one closed door.

And the world went black.

VIOLET

March turned out the light.

He turned out the light in the hallway. It wasn't agreed on. We hadn't planned it. He saw the switch and I suppose he thought of what we'd just talked about: darkness is safer. A click, and Ellie vanished in the dark.

We heard a door open. Boots.

March grabbed my arm before I could move towards the sound – towards where Ellie had been, towards where the boots were. He pulled me back into the stairway.

She'd been out in the hallway, in the open. I knew I couldn't get to her. I had one second to stop them from getting to her, instead.

I shouted, 'HERE,' along the hall, hearing the sound echo before March pulled me back, and we ran.

NINETEEN

PEACHES

I don't know how long I was alone in that room for. It's not that time was flying, it was more like it had stopped. My heartbeat, which had been so loud I was sure it would give me away, fell silent and still. Even my breathing was deadened by the velvet curtain, laying thick and heavy round me like a new sweep of snow. I stood there long enough to learn every snare in the fabric.

Eleven steps to come into the room. Twelve to leave. More as he passed along the hallway, checked into other rooms. In my snowed-under silence I counted him out of earshot and still didn't move.

I'd survived. I'd survived in the kind of childish hiding place I used to use when I was nine years old and didn't want to go to the school canteen by myself. The kind of hiding place I'd get hauled out of by teachers too used to my tricks, who'd seen my patent-leather shoes sticking out at the bottom of the curtain.

I survived because the drapes were thick enough to swamp even me.

And because the gunman had entered the room looking

185

for someone, and found a window open and a boy broken beneath. They didn't know there was anyone else to find.

Three times I'd survived.

Three times lucky. They never tell you what happens on time number four.

I didn't know if March and Joe were still alive or if fate had traded three lives for mine, a bargain even I would have said was a bad deal.

When I finally left, it was without looking out of the window. Something tugged in me to see for myself – something the counsellor they have us see likes to call closure – but I don't want to close that friendship. I know Moz died. I know that if I visit his house all I'll see are his features in the faces of his family. I know they're going through unimaginable loss. I know I'll never see him again.

But I do, when I close my eyes. I see him smiling, hair windswept as he leans back between gantry bars with his arms spread out like wings. And he's safe now. He's safe.

So I didn't look out of the window. But I knew if I stayed too long I wouldn't be able to resist.

I counted my steps to the door. Fifteen. And three more into the hallway.

Where someone was standing, more blood than boy.

JOE

It got so quiet when the shooting stopped.

They must have blown the lock off the door, because it opened under a kick. I heard, wasn't watching. I was flat on my back, Doug heavy and still against my chest. His blood was soaking through me. I hadn't thought he could have had that much left.

The last word I heard Sam say was 'Mum?'

He didn't lay back far enough. The bullet went straight through his throat, clipped his spine. Would have been quick.

His phone stayed on. It was his sister, not his mum, on the other end. I don't know how I recognised the voice: most of it was screaming. I just cursed it. Cursed everything, because it was going to pull their attention towards me. They were kicking bodies to test for signs of life as they walked into the room. I heard someone start whimpering, then the sound stopped with a shot.

And I thought about being dead. Kept my eyes closed, Doug's weight pressing down like earth shovelled over my chest, keeping my breaths short. Thought about the blood soaking my shirt as if it was my blood. Then I tried to stop thinking, blanking my mind of everything. Grief, fear, shame, guilt. I wouldn't be hungry again, or cold. No needs. No feelings. Dead.

The phone beside my head went dead. Unanswered.

I didn't feel relieved. I didn't feel. My body was slowly numbing and even when everything finally went quiet around me, I didn't move.

Eventually, people got up. Not many of them. Someone jostled me, crawling over Doug's legs. I didn't move. His body was still warm but his blood was starting to cool against my skin. I didn't know if it was all his any more.

If I could have wished myself dead, then I'd have done it.

I opened my eyes slowly.

They hadn't touched Sam's face. He'd have been glad about that. Vain bastard. I put out my hand and closed his eyes.

He wasn't stiff, or cold. Death doesn't look like sleep, not the way they tell you it does, but he looked on the verge of blinking awake. Or he would have, without the hole in his neck.

I wrapped my other arm round Doug's shoulders. No rise. No fall. He'd finally stopped bleeding.

I was just going to lay there with him, stay there with both of them until one of the shooters came back to end me, too. Only someone started crying – this boy started crying and it was the worst noise you've ever heard. And I could feel it echoing in my chest, that same sound, and I couldn't let it out. I wouldn't have stopped. I'd still be making that sound now.

What the hell good would that have done?

I crawled out of there. The shooting seemed like it was over, or maybe I wasn't listening any more. If I'd heard them firing in the rooms above I might have walked up there to meet them on purpose. As it was, I just walked. Up stairs, along halls, I didn't care where.

And then there she was.

PEACHES

His eyes were so blank that he was looking straight at me and I still wasn't sure he'd seen me at all.

JOE

It felt like I'd dreamed her. Pulled her back in with me when I knew she couldn't be. I'd seen her go.

PEACHES

'Joe?' I took a careful step towards him. He was soaked with blood, so much he looked like he'd just been dragged out of a river of it. I couldn't figure out how he was still standing.

JOE

She couldn't be there. If she was outside, then I could still think of her as safe.

PEACHES

'Are you . . .? Where are you hurt?' I touched his arm gently, as if I thought the slightest pressure could topple him over. His shirt clung like it had been pasted to him.

JOE

Her hands were cold.

PEACHES

I'd stood by that open window so long I was freezing again.

JOE

She was so cold. I remembered how she'd taken off the shirt I gave her to help Doug.

I looked down at her cold hands.

I slowly lifted mine and slid my fingers between hers.

VIOLET

We ran until we hit the ground floor, and March wanted to run further but I dug in my heels hard enough to stop both of us. We listened for echoes on the staircase.

The boots that had tracked us downwards had only come down one level. They were in retreat now, quieter

190

and slower with every step back up. Away from us. Towards Ellie.

'We have to go back for her.'

For a second it really was my intention to be the one giving chase this time. To run back up the stairs. I've rarely felt that kind of anger before. That night had been full of fear, but now I was angry for how frightened I had to be. I wanted to know where my mother and Ade were. I wanted to know Ellie was safe.

I wanted to know Ellie. In less than an hour she had moved from someone unreachable to someone I wanted to know every detail of. I wanted to know her long after the night was over.

'She has to live,' I told March urgently.

We all had to live.

'Of course she does,' he said. We left gaps between our words long enough to listen, so no one coming down could take us by surprise. 'So either we can go back up now and ask the people shooting at us very nicely if they'll let her sit this one out, or we hope your distraction worked.'

My distraction. I could still hear my voice expand to fill the hallway. I'm not usually so loud. It didn't even sound like mine.

March paused and listened.

I thought, *He looks so tired.*

'Thanks for that moment of sheer terror, by the way. But as a diversion tactic it was a good one.'

'There was no tactic to it,' I admitted.

'I know.' He pinched his lips together and added, 'She'll be fine. Inshallah, she knows where we were planning to go. So we could go there. Or we could go through one of the windows and get out of here right now.'

He said 'we' every time. I only realise when I go back through it. Always 'we', never the possibility that he would leave while I made the poorer choice. At school he always seemed to be alone, except for lessons. I checked the bookings for peer mentors and found he was the least requested, though he gets marks better than mine and with less effort. I'd seen him after school, with friends, but at Clifton he was always by himself.

And still, in the worst possible time, he saw himself as 'we'.

That's something it took me much longer to learn.

I did think about those windows. We could have left then, unobstructed except for the edges of the glass. But it would have put more distance between us and Ellie when there was already too much. I couldn't think of her looking for us to find we'd gone.

And I had no certain knowledge of what was waiting outside.

'We still have to go to the cellars. It's the only thing we can do that might help her.'

'Then you're ruling out asking nicely?' March asked, and I laughed despite everything. I could have cried as easily.

'For now.'

'Good,' he said. 'We have to keep something as a last resort.'

He gestured left. I shook my head, and we walked right.

'Have I mentioned,' he whispered, 'that I'm afraid of the dark?'

TWENTY

JOE

She said, 'We've got to get you somewhere safer,' and then flinched as I looked towards the room she'd come out of.

'Not there.'

Instead, she used my grip on her and her grip on my shoulder to push-pull me down the hallway to somewhere new. She was pushing hard for someone I still hoped I was dreaming. 'They've just been through here, so we might have some time before they come back.'

'Might' was about as optimistic as either of us could hope for.

Pressing me through a doorway and against the wall inside, out of sight, she pulled her hand away from my shoulder to put it on her hip. 'Now will you tell me where you're hurt?'

Too pissed off with me to be a dream, too. The state I was in I couldn't tell the difference between mad at me and afraid for me. But if she was real, then: 'Why the hell did you come back in?'

PEACHES

It was the first real sign of life he'd shown, so he could be angry with me all he wanted. I'd snapped at him first – all that blood and no obvious place it was coming from, and no answers on what I should be doing to help.

I didn't answer his question, though. Not honestly. 'I was missing your sweet nature so much I couldn't stay away.' If my voice hadn't hiccupped at the end I might have pulled off the deadpan. 'I left you with Ellie. You were supposed to be safe.'

JOE

The breath I drew in shook on my lips. 'No one's safe.'

With the hand tangled up in mine she reached out enough to draw the sodden hem of my shirt upwards, over my smooth uninjured stomach. Her voice got so soft I had to crane my head forward to hear. 'Where's the blood coming from, Joe?'

And I couldn't stop shaking then. It was in my voice, my hands. All through me. Down to my bones.

'It's Doug's.'

PEACHES

And for a few minutes, while he struggled to tell me the barest sketch of what happened, it felt like history repeating. Like I was stuck in a loop of watching boys fall apart.

ELLIE

I was stuck. That was the main thing I knew about where I'd ended up: I wouldn't be able to move from it for a while.

When the lights went out, I ran into the first room I could reach, my tights skidding along the polished floor. I heard the door to the next room open. It was dark in the hall but all the lights were still on everywhere else. If they'd seen me get in here, they'd find me.

Then I heard Violet. The stupid, brave, clever idiot shouted out, and I heard someone take off after her.

And I was frozen between choices. Should I run too, and which way? Go after March and Violet and whoever was chasing them? Call him back to run after me instead?

Or should I run the other way and stick to the plan, try to make it to the central staircase and meet them on the ground floor?

I did neither.

The floorboards in the next room creaked. A shout, local-accented, told everyone to get back against the windows. There were shuffling noises. I caught one quickly hushed sob.

At least I knew one thing now.

They had a plan.

PEACHES

I'm not saying I thought it was a *good* idea, with Joe in the state he was in, and after what had happened with Moz. Just that, by then, there weren't any good ideas left to have, and I only knew one place in the whole stupid stately home that didn't seem like it would be an obvious place to hide.

So we went to the roof.

My stomach was turning somersaults the whole way there. Every corner we turned I was sure would be the last one.

JOE

I just followed. I still . . . didn't really care what happened. I didn't care where she was taking me anyway. But I still had my fingers caught up with hers and sometimes I'd test the grip.

Just to make sure I could pull her back from something, if I needed to.

PEACHES

He'd almost stopped shaking. He never cried, just shook
like he was going to come apart. Crying might have helped,
I don't know, but we never had the time to cry for long
that night.

JOE

She said we were going upstairs. When we got there, it was
just this small, ordinary little doorway in an alcove off the
main hall. Ordinary apart from the push bar across it instead
of a handle, and the 'no exit or entry' sign.

PEACHES

Obviously, it was alarmed. Usually the instant the bar was
pushed some huge alert would ring through the house and
shake the security staff out of bed. But I knew I'd seen the
alarm panel flashing when we'd come in. Either everything
that could be triggered already had been, or if not, then one
more security alert getting issued to some far-off computer
couldn't possibly hurt.

I didn't know where the security guards were, but I
assumed they'd have gone to investigate at some point during
the fireworks, when the cheering turned to screams.

I assumed they weren't much defence against men
with guns, either.

JOE

She pushed the bar down. Nothing happened except the door swinging open on to a small windy outside space.

And I mean, the world already felt upside down, so going outside from the top floor of a house didn't seem as weird as it might have. The rush of cold air made me feel awake again as I followed her out, letting the door swing and click shut behind us.

'What's this?'

PEACHES

'The roof.'

It was a small courtyard, maybe a quarter of the size of the rooms below, with walls to about waist height surrounding it on three sides. On the other, another section of roof sloped up at an angle over the window and flattened out again on the other side.

This was where Moz and I had escaped to air the sweat off our skin after being stuck in the overheated ballroom for the Christmas show.

Moz had loved it out there.

I planned to keep Joe as far from the edge as possible.

JOE

'Part of the roof, anyway,' Peaches said, turning around and splaying out her palms like an estate agent showing off the space. It kept me from moving too far forward. 'They come up here to do the pigeon-proofing.'

PEACHES

'Pigeon-proofing,' Joe repeated slowly.

ELLIE

I got in a cupboard. Something that might have held spare linen or folded clothes when the room was really a bedroom, and now sat empty in one corner of the room. There was just enough space below the lowest shelf for me to fold myself inside, knees up to my chest as I stuck my fingers through the slatted door and pulled it closed after me.

I heard the man who'd run off after Violet coming back. Or maybe it was the third gunman coming to join the others. I had no way of knowing, but I could hear him step into each room to check it as he approached.

He stepped into mine.

And moved on.

There was a short conversation in the next room, too low for me to make out the words. There was no other sound, but I knew there must be other people in there. They'd been given orders.

Hostages?

My phone buzzed in my pocket. In surprise I banged my head on the shelf above me and then sat as still as I could, praying it wasn't enough to be overheard. With just one hand I got hold of my phone, glancing at the screen as I went to turn it off.

The display said: *DAD*.

PEACHES

Pigeon-proofing. It's something old houses have to do to stop themselves ending up with rafters full of flapping, crapping house guests. Every so often they hire people to come out to put up nets, or spikes, and clean and repaint the bits the pigeons did manage to get to.

I told Joe all the comparatively few facts I knew about it, reasoning that talking about something boring and a little bit gross was better than going over everything we'd both been through.

They make you talk about it a lot, when you've been through trauma. I don't know how much it helps. I'm talking it through for you now, because I have to, because everyone says how important it is to add my voice to all the others, to speak for the ones who can't. But really, I'd take pigeons over terrorists any day. And I don't even like them, much.

JOE

I still don't know what she was talking about, but it helped. Listening to her instead of the inside of my head helped. The voice that had been alternating between telling me to survive however I could or just give up had shut off, and it was just her and me for a while.

I was back to myself enough to notice that the cold that had helped wake me up was biting into her exposed skin. She was still in a vest and culottes, practically nothing.

Couldn't exactly suggest popping back in to warm up.

'You look freezing. You can stand with me, if you want.'

PEACHES

He opened his arms. I *was* freezing, but I looked at his blood-soaked shirt, still damp, and chewed on my lip.

'Not really?'

ELLIE

DAD.

I couldn't stop myself. I pressed to accept the call.

I needed it not to be a trick or mistake. It was worth the risk just to make sure it was really him on the other end of the line.

'Ellie, Ellie, where are you? We got your messages. Where are you? Are you safe?'

It was. It was really my dad. He sounded desperate, and his voice cracked wide open on the word 'safe', but he was alive. And he'd said 'we'.

'Tell me whe—'

I hung up.

Before the buzz of his voice gave me away, or I gave in to the sobs that were clogging up my throat just from hearing it, I hung up the phone. And twice more while I was frantically typing.

Can't talk now text me love you so much daddy
Is mum ok are you

Trying to keep any part of me focused somewhere other than my phone was difficult, but I tried to listen to the footsteps in the next room, so I'd know if the faint vibration of texts coming in had attracted attention. In my small, cramped space each one felt like it a little earthquake. He sent two messages back.

We r safe. Police r here, tell me where you r they will find you.

Love you, love you, love you.

Police. Finally. I felt like I could have burst out of the cupboard just from knowing. One room away from men with guns and hostages, I felt safe again.

Police!!
I've been so scared

I'm in the house

It was longer before I got a message in return this time. I watched the clock at the top of my phone for two long, painful minutes before I tried again.

Hello?

Then Dad got back to me, just three words.

Inside Hearne House?

I tapped out a confirmation.

Yes tell the police

There are lots of us here

And he didn't reply for a long time.

TWENTY-ONE

TESTIMONY OF SIMEON BURNETT, POLICE SERGEANT: AMBERSIDE STATION

You don't generally need body armour working for a small-town police station in a division made up of other small towns and satellite villages. I get officers needing wellington boots to retrieve sheep blocking muddy roads more often than I get requests for protective gear. There are the usual annoyances, the problem drug users, petty thieves, drunks who like to use the station as a roof over their heads for the night. Domestic violence isn't unusual. Car accidents happen. I can count the murder cases on one hand.

Terrorism? There's an army barracks not far out of Amberside, and a MOD base where they can practise blowing things up far enough out not to disturb anybody. A decent number of the military kids go to local schools. Ambereve Festival functions as a fundraiser for the military benevolent fund. That night it was the only thing I could think of that might have made us a target. But you'd never expect it in a small town. When they talk about critical terror alerts, you don't think they mean you. Don't think it means this. No one could have predicted it.

They sent in firearms officers from the city. Negotiators from the regional CTU. The army barracks were alerted, too. The time it took to coordinate and get people in place felt like giving them free rein behind those walls.

I drove up. I could hear some of the shots.

We had clearance to bring a helicopter in, but landing it was too much of a concern when we had a dark field strewn with people.

I briefed the officers and medics who'd got out of their beds to join us. By then half the town was awake trying to get up the hill to look for their kids. There was field medicine being practised along the parade route. Some of them were even forcing their way inside to track down loved ones.

I deployed a good section of my force on crowd control, so we could get ambulances through. Stalling frightened people with very little information or reassurance to offer isn't the easy job it sounds. It was hard enough to keep my officers from breaking ranks and going in. Some of them did and I won't blame them.

The rest of us suited up in protective gear. Once we had clearance to enter the grounds we'd be in like a shot. I can't tell you the frustration in waiting.

Finally we had the hostages by the car recovered without casualty. One of the hostage takers was down, the other injured but alive. People were getting out again over the bridge. Getting them clear became our priority.

After that, we heard about the local bulldozing efforts. A couple of farmers using their vehicles to bring down a section of the exterior wall. It was half help, half hinderance, if I'm honest – we had more well-intentioned folk getting into the grounds when they'd have done better to stay well clear. But I'll say this for them: it meant special forces could get vehicles through quick. That action saved lives. It felt like things were swinging our way about then.

Then we got word that there were more hostages in Hearne House. And the men with them had explosives.

* * * * * * * * * * *

TWENTY-TWO

PEACHES

He rubbed his hands over my arms. Which I told him I could have done for myself, but he ran one hand down to press his palm to mine and shook his head. 'Your hands are cold too.'

Joe's hands were warm. They felt too warm against my skin, but then I was probably a few degrees away from hypothermia by that point. It was like the cold was freezing my brain into inactivity. He can't have been warm, either, in that soaked shirt. I hate that one of the things I know now is that blood doesn't stay heated for long. You need to keep it inside your body for that.

Another thing I know: dead people don't bleed. Blood doesn't flow without a heartbeat pushing it along. So when I read the reports of how people were found, I can tell more easily than I'd like to who died slow and who went quick.

JOE

'You shouldn't be out here,' I muttered, knowing the other choices were limited at best. I couldn't warm her up with just two palms, but I smoothed them back up to her shoulders, just in case.

PEACHES

I'd finally forgotten to feel self-conscious about my body at some point during the million years between getting shot at by the river and ending up here. Amazing what it takes to shift the dumbest of priorities. Now, after everything that happened, I'm not sure I could remember how to feel self-conscious if I tried. We weren't dead, and just then having a body still capable of function and movement, of pumping blood – that wasn't anything I could be ashamed of.

'Nobody should be here.' I ducked my head until it came to rest against his shoulder. I was too afraid to be tired, but exhausted all the same. 'But I can go in and ask if they want to relocate the whole mass murder thing to somewhere with better central heating, if you like.'

VIOLET

Opening the door to the cellars below the building, we were met by a sigh of cool air rushing to greet us. The further down, the colder it would get. I looked up at March, who was afraid of the dark, and took the first step down myself.

There was a switch on the wall. Pressing it down flicked on a string of narrow bars of light all the way down the

209

bottom. 'There. Now it's only the way back you'll have to worry about.'

'I'm starting to think we need to go back to keeping torches somewhere other than our phones,' he said, closing the door with a faint click as he followed me.

'What happened to yours?'

'It was in my pocket.' He pushed a hand into the front pocket of his shirt and wiggled a finger through a hole I had not looked closely enough to notice before. Right over his heart.

'A phone stopped a bullet?' I had seen the damage it could do to the soft tissue of human flesh. To be halted by a small package of metal and wire seemed incredible.

March made a sudden study of the stone slabs on the floor. 'It was slowed down by the girl in front of me, first.'

Then I understood. As words still seemed better than silence, I changed the questions that I asked. 'Is there anyone that you need to call? When we find Ellie again – she has a phone.'

He was quiet for a moment, then hurried down the steps ahead of me. 'No. Everyone I know is fine.'

PEACHES

I was still considering the cold. 'Though, to be fair, they did plan all this around a bonfire. It's not their fault we didn't stay put . . . What are you doing?'

JOE

I squeezed her hands and let them go, stepping around her to walk over to one of the walls. It was her mentioning the Welcome Fire. I just – for some reason I needed to know if it was still burning. 'I'm just going to see what's happening.'

She grabbed my elbow, and – Peaches is a girl who refuses to look scared most of the time, even when she's being shot at – but she did then. 'I don't think it'll be much of a view.'

I moved forward anyway. We were too high and too far to see much of anything, but the fire was still there, bleeding white smoke into the black air. Peaches wouldn't get close to the wall. She was still dragging at my elbow, her heels set into the ground. I frowned back at her.

'Is there any reason you think I need an anchor?'

The wall came up higher than my hip. It wasn't like there was a risk of tripping, so I asked, 'Do I look like I'm about to jump?'

PEACHES

I jerked back hard. The jerk finally moved with me, taking a full step away from the wall. It felt like someone had reconnected my oxygen supply.

'No one does, until right before they do.'

'Maybe it's an option, though,' he said. The dick, the *idiot*. 'Might be preferable to whatever they have in mind.'

My nails dug into his skin and I was glad when he flinched. 'No, you know what's preferable? *Not dying's* preferable. Even when it's a choice between probably dying one way and definitely dying the other, you need to take the option that's only probably every time. You're seventeen years old. Do you know how many years dying now would *waste*?'

JOE

'All right, Jesus. Try not to rip my skin off.' She looked like all the ghosts of the day were waiting on the other side of that high wall, and maybe she was right. 'I've been told I'm a waste of space before, never the opposite. Anyway, it was a joke. A shit one, obviously, but I swear I'm not about to jump.'

PEACHES

'Any more jokes like that and I'll be tempted to push you. Don't.'

He tried to put an arm round me. I ducked down and away.

JOE

So I just stood there, one arm out, like a lemon. 'You're not like most girls, are you?'

She sniffed. 'No girl is like most girls. That's because girls aren't a homogeneous mass.'

I let my arm slap down to my side, and laughed. I *laughed*. 'See, that's what I mean.'

PEACHES

'No, you mean I'm not like you think girls are supposed to be.' I ran my hands over my arms as if I could brush off his touch. 'And I'd say I was sorry about that but, firstly, I'm not, and, secondly, it would take a lot more than a blonde wig and some platform heels to turn me into someone like Ellie Kimber.'

JOE

It was all so out of the blue I stuttered for a moment before I could even reply.

'Who says I'd want you to be like Ellie?'

The eyeroll she gave me was impressive all on its own. 'I know the way you look at her.'

I had a sudden flash of memory. Watching Ellie Kimber dance. The way she shone in the night. Sam and Doug laughing, hardly bothering to act like they weren't watching, too. I gave myself a minute to hope that, once the gunmen had finished with us, they hadn't gone upstairs for Ellie.

'How do you know?' I asked slowly.

Before that night I hadn't known Peaches at all. Although apparently she'd known me. I can't make excuses, other than Sam, Doug and me have probably made shitty comments about half the school at one time or another. It's what we do.

Did.

PEACHES

I spun back to stare at him. 'Because it's the same way *everyone* looks at her.'

It was the way precisely no one ever looked at me. As soon as I'd said it I was shaking my head, pushing the palms of my hands against my face. Not the time or the place or the person to be inviting to your pity party, Peaches. I really could make everything about me. I was halfway through saying sorry, it wasn't important, when Joe nodded his head a fraction and said, 'Yeah, I guess I do look at her. Not the way you think, though. She's just – she's everything I want.'

Which was *exactly* the way I'd thought, and I was about to say so. He put his hands up to stop me interrupting. Rephrased.

'I mean, she's everything I want to be.'

JOE

'You want to be a gorgeous blonde with a lingerie sponsorship?' Peaches asked.

I wasn't putting any of this well. Why would I, though? I'd never said it before. And no one else had asked. 'She just gets taken so seriously. Her parents drive her to training every morning at six a.m. Did you know that? If I see her, it's because I'm trying to get a quick run in down the park road before anyone else is awake enough to see me. She's on the Olympic track. I'm in the mud in Primarni trainers.'

PEACHES

'I didn't know you did athletics.' The only time I saw Joe Mead near the games field was when he was smoking behind the changing rooms. And that wasn't very athletic behaviour, either.

'I don't. I used to.' He stared down at his feet. 'I used to be good.'

'So what happened?'

'Don't know. I grew up and you're not supposed to take it seriously any more. Dad had all these issues with it, so he was never going to start getting up in the dark to get me to the track. He was never going to come and stand proudly at every event the way the Kimbers do. And my friends weren't about to stay that way if I was training twelve-hour days. No drinking, nothing.'

I almost suggested that they can't have been very good friends. The thing is, he never asked them to be. Now they won't have a chance to show him he was wrong.

'You were keeping up appearances,' I said. And I thought that maybe if I'd ever had the right appearance, I'd have done anything to keep it, too.

I said, 'You're not a waste of space.'

And I stepped back into his.

He looked at me. He pressed his hands to the small of my back, folded there like a prayer. Then the lights below us all went out.

VIOLET

I found the electrical panel and March pulled the cover open to get to the main circuit breaker and flipped it to off. That done, he ran his fingers down the switches for each part of the house and set them to off, too, working blind in the sudden, engulfing black.

'Should we stay down here, now?' March asked. I heard him step back from the panel. One more step and he'd crash into me.

'We can't. We have to make sure Ellie is safe. And they'll know where we are now. If they want the light back, someone will come down before long.'

I could hear his breathing, nervous and noisy. With all that had happened, the dark was still frightening him.

'I don't know how we're supposed to find our way anywhere else.' His voice broke.

'March.' This wasn't the logical boy from my classes. I took his hand and pressed it to the wall. All we'd have to do was follow the line of it. 'Like this.'

TWENTY-THREE

ELLIE

Dad?

I was sending out another unanswered message when the light that had been filtering in through the cupboard door died. I didn't move, but there was a commotion coming through the wall.

Heavy footsteps strode into the hall. I could just about pick them out from the rest of the noise, which sounded more like a sudden flurry of small steps and shifting feet. I wondered if the hostages thought this was their chance to get past their captors. If the bullets might miss their backs in the dark.

It must have been what their captors were wondering, too. There was a single shot. I heard the rubble from the ceiling crash down.

When it settled, things were still again, although not silent. Two male voices countered each other in low rumbles. I couldn't make out words but the tone was firm. It sounded like a decision being made.

After they were done, a foot stamped down hard, like an order.

All I could think of was Violet and March. They'd done it. They were alive.

VIOLET

'In the fridges? They're big enough.'

We had reached the kitchen and a number of limited options had presented themselves. In the dark, everything that we touched was cold. Stainless-steel counters ran wall to wall and huge metal fridges and chest freezers loomed out as we got close to them. March had lifted the lid of one of the chests to be hit with an arctic blast.

'And they can't be opened from the inside. We would freeze to death, even with the power turned off.' I tutted, sucking the inside of my teeth. I sound like my mother when I do that.

A fragment of light shone in through the glass panels in the back door. I thought it must be the bonfire's glow, a far-off pinprick of heat. With heavy bars bolted across it, it looked like no one had been in or out this way yet. 'If we could get this open, we could go . . .' I said, before I'd thought of anything more than the possibility that my family, and safety, might be waiting on the other side. I'd almost forgotten how it had felt to be hunted through the open spaces out there.

I heard March turn towards me, and I remembered myself. 'When Ellie finds us, then we could go.'

He went back to feeling along the counters. 'OK. So, until then, I think there's some space under here.'

I was crouching down to see what he meant, when the shot rang out somewhere above our heads.

PEACHES

The shot rang out from the level below.

'That sounded like it was right beneath us.' It had been quiet for so long that the noise made me startle hard, my quick, nervous breaths turning to steam in the crisp air. All the lights that had cast a glow outward from the house were gone now. Even the tiny security light up here had died. I didn't know why, but every noise was louder in the dark.

I realised I was close enough to feel that Joe's heart was drumming as quick as mine.

He kept his voice to a hard whisper. 'It wasn't. It was at least two rooms along, but it was close.'

JOE

Peaches bowed her head to my shoulder. 'It's starting again.'

Of course it was. That was the only reliable thing I knew any more. When it went quiet, or seemed distant, it wasn't over. I knew by then that they were just taking time to reload or change their weapons over. It was always going to start again. They couldn't break me by letting me hope.

I rubbed a hand across her shoulders, smoothed my fingers through the tangles of her hair. I could hear Sam's voice overlaid with mine. 'We'll be OK. We'll be OK.'

She looked up at me. I found myself whispering it against her mouth.

ELLIE

There was a new set of footsteps coming along the hallway. Number three?

When he went through the door to the next room, the urge to get out and run was almost impossible to resist. I had to remind myself that three shooters were all we'd accounted for. It didn't mean that was all there were. Still, the idea of a free run along the hall back to the stairs and down to Violet would have won me over eventually, if there hadn't been something else going on.

The hostages were being moved. I couldn't count the footsteps or guess how many there might be, but it sounded like the clatter of a class getting up to change rooms at the sound of the bell.

My phone, finally, vibrated in my pocket, but I left it there for now, screwing my eyes closed to listen. Maybe this would give me a chance, after all.

VIOLET

'Do you think they're coming?' I asked March, pressed into the small, cold space beside me.

'I always think they're coming,' he said.

PEACHES

The truth is, no one had ever kissed me before Joe. I'd never kissed anyone. Up until that night my worst fear would have been taking that risk and having the other person pull away.

Can you even imagine something as small and insignificant as rejection being a person's worst fear? There are so many more terrible things in the world.

And Joe wasn't rejecting me. He kissed me like it was a request.

JOE

You're not getting the details on this. It just happened – we both needed something, and it turned out it was that. It turned out what I needed was her.

We had, like, three minutes before the door banged open and we both nearly fell straight over the edge.

ELLIE

I had my hand pressed up against the cupboard door, but I wasn't sure any more if I was trying to hold it closed or push it open. In my head I tried to replot the layout of the room I'd hidden in. I planned the quickest route from where I was to the door.

Through the wall I heard shuffling feet. A voice snapped, 'Stay together.'

It really could have been an unruly classroom.

By then most of the group must have been bunched up in the hall.

Then people started running. I heard a small stampede break off towards the central staircase, turning my head to follow the sound. Shots rang out, three of them, but there was still pounding on the staircase, heading up.

I was nearly sure I heard two of the shooters go after them, but it was so hard to keep track. Other people were moving now, scattering. The noise was everywhere, untraceable and impossible to pick out. There was chaos in the hallway, in the dark, but I knew where I needed to go.

I kicked my way out of the cupboard and ran into the hall, trusting instinct and memory to get me through.

VIOLET

It had been Ellie. That single shot was written with her name, somehow I was sure of it. I could feel it. The sense of loss was like a blow to the centre of my chest. We should have gone back for her. We should have stayed together. I whispered as much to March until he clasped my hands and hushed me. 'Don't put so much faith in yourself,' he said. 'Feelings aren't facts. Human brains just want things in order, that's all. They tell lies to you when they don't have enough information to tell the truth.'

It sounded like something our biology teacher would have said, while he ran a laser pen across a diagram of the hemispheres of the brain. I think it may actually have been that.

'What if the truth is nothing I want to know?' I asked, as the sound of running, hammering feet pounded above us.

PEACHES

The little rooftop had shrunk to feel just big enough for the two of us pressed together. Now suddenly five new people came crowding through the exit door. Seven. More. A girl was hysterical, screaming and crying. She climbed up on the edge of the wall. I screamed and swore and two people near her hooked her down. They were all talking at once.

He's coming.

Shit, shit, they're going to kill us, shit.

224

What did they want us for? Us. What did they want
us for?

I thought he was going to –

Have you seen Stephen?

What was he wearing under his vest?

The conversations were impossible to follow, though I
did pick up in a short space of time that they'd been held
somewhere silently, and now the last twenty minutes of their
terror was spilling noisily everywhere.

I also picked up that this small patch of rooftop wasn't
much of a hiding place any longer.

JOE

The shots didn't come from where I expected. As soon as
we'd been gatecrashed I was watching the door – I'd grabbed
Peaches' forearm and was trying to work the both of us as
far away from it as I could, over to the wall. Wasn't easy in a
mash of panicked people.

Then two shots came upwards, skimming the edge
of the courtyard wall by millimetres, and everyone pushed
back inwards.

'I can hear you.'

That's all he said. It was only time I heard his voice that
night, but I'll never forget how it sounded. Like a singsong,
like when you're playing with little kids and tell them *Here I*
come, ready or not.

225

Only he wasn't playing.

Ready or not. He knew where we were, so we had to be ready. In the suddenly empty corner of the courtyard, I leant out over the wall.

Obviously Peaches tried to heft me back, kicking at me and digging in her nails. 'No. *No*, we're not taking that way out,' she said.

'Just look, will you?' I pulled her forward so she could see what I was looking at, set into one of the indents between the windows of the house. Steps. Metal ones, with a narrow handrail, all painted a muted colour to blend in with the brickwork of the house.

I'd noticed them earlier, but wouldn't have remembered them now, except for the faint reflection of the bonfire catching on a few spots of scratched, exposed metal.

There actually was a way out. We'd just have to go over the wall.

TWENTY-FOUR

ELLIE

This is the church, this is the steeple, run down the hall and past all the people. It's not how the rhyme goes, I know, but I often have words in my head when I run: nursery rhymes, scraps of music, even something I might have overheard that day that's been trapped in my head ever since. The right words have a beat, and the right beat goes from my brain to my legs and keeps them moving.

Has she had a real boyfriend the whole time she's here? Nah, don't think so. I heard she's queer.

London Bridge is falling down, falling down, falling down.

Falling back on an old favourite, *Wait For It* from Hamilton, I cut myself off before I reached the part about death not discriminating over who it takes. It hit too sharp a nerve. Whatever was coming, I wasn't going to wait for it. *Wait for it. Wait for it.*

I kept hold of the beat in my head, and let my feet hit every stroke. The hallway was a muddled scrum. Two people rushing past almost turned me around right away, then a door to my left slammed shut. I didn't know who was behind it. It was like running with my eyes closed. I thought of the way I'd come slowly and carefully, checking every room, and I let my feet follow their own steps back until I hit the narrow staircase at the end. There were others running down ahead of me, some of them giving in to uncertainty and turning to go up.

'It's a dead end,' I called to faces I couldn't see as they passed me. 'There's nowhere to go at the top.'

I think they turned back again. I can't be sure. I wasn't counting anything but steps. Down, down, trying to think where Violet would be waiting. The power was off. It would be dangerous to stay in the cellars. Then where? Would she have got out? Part of me hoped she had and part of me knew there was no way she'd have left without me.

I could still hear her voice echoing down the hall after me. *HERE*.

Where was she?

I was almost there, halfway down the last flight of steps, when the tide turned against me. Suddenly people were fighting their way back up.

'They're down there. They're there. *Run.*'

I was running already. I'd trusted my feet to get me out of this, the way they'd got me everywhere. But as a crack of gunfire shook the walls, so loud and so close – as the boy one step up from me crumpled down into my arms – I knew I'd run the wrong way.

Now there was someone waiting at the bottom of the

steps for us, and someone else at the top.

We stood there, packed into that narrow, black staircase, and waited.

VIOLET

There was nothing to do but wait until the sounds of chaos above us softened and grew distant. The trouble was not over, I knew that, but it was on the move.

March and I were not. We knelt under the metal kitchen counter and he held my hands, or perhaps I held his. It was very dark. There was nothing to do but wait or run, and my legs felt too shaky to carry me.

There was another single shot. 'The other side of the house,' whispered March, and it grew quieter still.

And then we heard them coming.

ELLIE

They told us to walk. That wasn't what I'd expected. Penned in we made easy targets. I hadn't thought we'd be given another chance.

One of us didn't get his. The boy who'd fallen into me after that first warning shot sank down on to a step, unable to walk. 'Please,' he whispered, more air than sound, 'tell my mum. Tell my mum about me.'

I felt the moment he died. Even in the dark. It was like a candle blowing out.

His name was Andrew Wright. They printed his name with the lists of all the others, and read it out at the start of this inquest, but it wasn't until I saw the map of the house, with those red pins stuck through it to mark each life lost, that I could match the name to where he'd died.

I spoke to his mother last night for the first time. She told me he went to Sefton College. He was studying to be an aircraft engineer. She said he'd always been so smart, always believed he could take on the world. He was nineteen.

I told her about him, too. The little that I knew. He'd been behind me and hadn't shoved his way forward to put other people closer to danger like some of the rest. His body took a bullet that could have been for any one of us. He died without crying. His hair was so soft. She was the last thing in his thoughts.

There was a gun at our backs and we had no choice except to walk. We left Andrew there, sitting back against the step, with his cheek resting against the wall and a bullet in him that, with uncanny aim, had broken up inside one of the pathways to his heart.

The rest of us went on. There were chances for escape teasing me at every step of the march along the hallway on the ground floor. The corners of my eyes caught them: my subconscious made a note of every open door, every window framed with broken glass and open to the night.

No one ran. Our minds reached out for freedom but our bodies had learned the price of it. None of us could outrun bullets.

'Walk,' the man behind us said, with one of his heavy-booted stamps that underlined the order. 'Just keep walking and we won't shoot you.'

I wish I could have looked round. I wish it hadn't been so dark. I wanted to know if the man holding a gun at the back of our small line was the same one whose blue eyes had caught mine in the crowd in front of the stage.

They marched us through to the kitchens and stood us in a line of eleven or twelve, while one of them worked on forcing open the barred kitchen door. There was a light flickering in the frosted glass of the door panel. Not orange, like the fire, but blue.

How long ago had Violet asked if I'd heard sirens? She'd heard better than me.

I guessed at the rest of their plan then. They weren't going to shoot us, that was true. They'd let the police do that.

VIOLET

I have looked up how long a person can hold their breath for. Only thirty seconds on average. Perhaps two minutes for the very fit. Seven in unusual cases, such as divers who live half their lives underwater, their metabolisms slowed by the cold.

It was cold then. But it felt as though I stopped breathing from the moment that those feet marched through and lined up along the counter in front of us. I could see the backs of their legs: skirts, trousers, trainers, jeans, everything monochrome to my poorly adjusted eyes. Crouching low in our hiding place I held and held my breath, biting down on the inside of my cheeks to keep my teeth from chattering with the chill of fear.

March's fingers were curled round my wrist, and I have often wondered if he felt my pulse stop. It felt as though my heart gave up beating for as long as they stood there.

Could I see Ellie? I tried. It seemed to me that I *should* know her, that the presence that marked her out as unique should extend right down even to the backs of her calves. But all I saw were feet shifting, nerves twitching through muscles, terror played out in the small motions of a dozen pairs of unidentifiable legs.

ELLIE

The padlock from the door hit the ground with a metallic ring. Someone yelped, and then clamped both hands over her mouth to seal in the sound. I could still hear the cry trying to escape from between her fingers.

A phone buzzed into life, to be answered quickly by the gunman at the door. 'Yeah,' he said. 'We're ready to talk.'

There was something about his voice. I didn't believe him.

And there was no more talking, not then. I knew he'd hung up because the phone was buzzing again, this time given no answer.

Back then, I wanted to hear what they wanted. I wanted to know the point they were trying to make. *Why* they were there. More than anything I wanted to know the reason that so many of us had to die for whatever cause they were carrying around with them, locked in the chambers of their rifles and hidden under their thick black vests. As if there really could be something to explain – to justify what they'd done. As if there might be some way that we had deserved it. My therapist's right. I really am good at putting blame in all the wrong places.

Now, I don't want to listen to their reasons at all. We shouldn't give them our breath. It's like Violet says: there's no *reason* in any of this.

But that unanswered phone made me feel crazy, then.

I felt for the phone in my own pocket, relieved that I'd remembered to switch it off. But the one who'd stood guarding us saw the movement and jammed the hilt of his rifle into my shoulder. My phone skidded across the floor as I bent double with the pain.

And, even as I knew it could be worse, I watched his heel come down on the screen, and it made me ache even more. I had to put Dad out of my mind. I had to forget the relief I'd heard in his voice for those couple of seconds when he'd thought I was safe.

Most of all, I had to not react to the brief but certain glimpse I'd caught of two people huddled together under the metal counter.

VIOLET

She saw us. I wouldn't have been sure of it except for the slight gasp she gave, a moment too late for it to be a response to her own pain.

As for Ellie, even in the dark she stood out like a beacon. Until she bent forward she'd been just out of the line of my vision, and I realised then I should have been looking for someone without shoes.

He had hit her with the gun, I thought, which was better than the alternative, but still made me want to crawl out of my hiding place and ask how he dared. I looked at March instead. His eyes shone, the brightest thing I could see there. The three of us, still alive.

And then the two men with them were giving orders. The hostages were to walk ahead of them, with their hands on their heads. Move their hands, and they would be shot. Try to run towards the police, and they would be shot in the back.

The police. The police were here. Surely it meant that all this would soon be over. Our hunters were giving themselves up. Surely it meant that my mother and Ade would have been found and taken somewhere safe.

But it was not over yet, and to lose something precious in the last possible second would be the worst loss of all. The twelve in the line in front of us followed the orders they had been given. I watched their hands lift from their sides before they started a slow walk towards the door. I wanted to be with them, to follow them, to be among the first into the arms of rescue, but I made myself wait.

The door opened. One by one, they filed through. There was a noise from far beyond the door, the crackle of amplified speech through a loudhailer. I think it must have been an attempt to make contact.

Then the gunfire came thick and fast.

TWENTY-FIVE

ELLIE

'ARMED POLICE.'

I stepped through the back door and had maybe three seconds to take in what waited outside.

Second one: we weren't completely exposed. There was a stone wall a few steps ahead of us that came to waist height, separating the path at the back of the house from the kitchen gardens.

'ARMED POLICE. GET ON YOUR KNEES NOW. DROP YOUR WEAPONS NOW.'

Second two: there was a line of police officers gathered opposite, standing about as far away as one side of Amberside high street is from the other. They weren't exposed, either. They must have cleared the bridge and managed to get cars and vans in. They stood behind a blockade of them. They had shields and grey uniforms, with helmets and scarves across their faces that made them look like paler echoes of the men behind us.

'DROP YOUR WEAPONS. DROP YOUR –'

Second three: the police were panicking. The shooters hadn't arranged this – no one expected them to leave the

236

house without negotiating. They'd known the police weren't going to start shooting with a row of hostages lined up in front of them.

The fourth second was when the first bullet came over my shoulder. Our captors had no such qualms.

All of us dropped to the ground. It was as though the *get on your knees* had been meant for us. It wasn't what they wanted, of course. As soon as their human shield buckled, the police could fire back. I closed my eyes and saw fireworks exploding over my head.

PEACHES

We hadn't been the first people to find the fire escape that night. Broken windows as we climbed down showed it had been an entry point we just hadn't seen before. I couldn't believe I hadn't realised there would be one. It was a huge old building built before fire codes and regulations. Of course they'd have updated the escape routes along with the toilets and kitchens, and whatever else the Tudors just left to chance.

It was narrow, though, and certainly not built to have five people hanging off it at once. Joe had taken the first step out into the unknown, and above me the rest of the panicked strangers from the rooftop were dangling legs over the wall and hopping out. Every time the metal framework gave a new jerk, I looked up to see someone safely holding on, and took another breath.

I've never had a problem with heights. I like feeling closer to the sky than the earth. But now every step made me flinch in case the stairs gave way under me, or under someone above. Every time I looked down I half expected to see Joe falling away from the wall below me.

Instead, I looked across the field and saw blue lights streaking towards the house.

JOE

There were lights, but the sirens had been hushed, and the cars took an odd zigzag path. I think they must have been going around bodies. Somehow they were coming in from the back of the field, instead of over the bridge.

I wasn't sure what it meant. It was too dark to see officers on foot slowly clearing the edges of the field, securing one small square at a time, going in teams so that no one took on the threat alone. But I knew they must be massing where they'd assessed the worst danger still was. And that meant surrounding the house.

'We're going to have to run for it,' I called up to Peaches, watching her foot grope for the next step and slowly settle flat before she put her weight on it. 'Get to the police if we can, or just out into the grounds.'

She'd been right, all along. Entering Hearne House in the first place had been the worst mistake.

PEACHES

'We'll get to the ground and run,' I called upwards, hoping someone would listen and pass it on. The night wind whipped half my voice away from me before it could get anywhere, but I could hear the choke in my voice. 'The police are here.'

We're taught, when we're little, that if you're in trouble you find a policeman. My mum tells a story about 'the first time I was brought home by the police' – when I was four. I'd managed to walk the two streets to the local park alone, and was trying to charm strangers into buying me a bag of birdseed from a stand by the water that offered overpriced snacks for both people and ducks.

When I was done, I just walked up to a policewoman making her rounds and asked her to take me home.

Mum laughs about opening the door and saying she didn't expect to be hearing from the police about me until I was in my teens. She says she thought I was in the garden. She'd just popped in to catch the end of her TV show. But I must have been gone for at least an hour by then.

Anyway, the same way I knew the rule when I was four, I knew it now. When you're in trouble, you find a police officer.

As I hurried my steps a little to get down, I felt so ready to go home.

JOE

They were parking up a short run away from the house. Getting out, forming a wall.

Below us, a door opened I didn't even know was there.

And then the world went screeching back to hell.

VIOLET

'They're shooting them!'

I'd flown out of our hiding space in the second that the door had been kicked closed in their wake. That felt to me like a signal. That they'd closed off their means of escape, or retreat, made whatever was happening beyond that door feel final. They weren't coming back. And I didn't know what ending they intended to bring about.

March caught my arm as I reached for the handle. 'They're shooting at the police.' He was on the balls of his feet, trying to squint the frosted glass into focus. 'They need them as a human shield.'

But shields take the brunt of damage. And how many did they have with them? I'd counted twelve. If one, or two, or five were lost to stray bullets, how soon before the police counted the shield as a necessary sacrifice to end this and save however many of us were still hidden inside the house?

I turned back to March. I told him to hide, if he had to.

'I can't leave her,' I said.

So I opened that door.

PEACHES

They were firing at the police from one level below our feet.
Suddenly the spot where we'd planned to jump from the fire
escape and run to safety became the kind of spot you'd only
aim for if you had a real craving for a bullet in your back.

I spared a millisecond to run through every obscenity
I knew.

Then I looked up to see the third shooter firing from
above. He'd made it to the rooftop we'd abandoned. It
would've been the perfect vantage point for picking us off the
fire escape like bottles off a wall, if it wasn't also the perfect
vantage point for shooting over the police defences and
straight into their ranks. I saw them huddle, trying to defend
with their shields in two directions at once.

It felt like I'd guess a warzone must feel. And some
nights I still dream that I'm stuck there listening to the
gunfire, unending, day to day, night to night.

JOE

We made for the closest windows. For Peaches and me that
meant the ground floor. I went through first and got a knee
full of broken glass trying to help her in after me. I didn't
feel it until I had hold of both her hands and we hit the
floor inside.

Still alive, still alive. Somehow still alive.

ELLIE

They dragged a few of us back to our feet. I opened my eyes
and looked up to see one of them holding a girl against his
chest because she couldn't stand on her own. Eventually he
dropped her and ordered more of us to get up, waving the
handgun he was feeding a new cartridge into. We could die
on our knees or take the chance of surviving standing.

I was near the end of the line. I chose to die on my feet.
Slowly, I made my limbs coordinate. Pushed my hand into
the ground and got my ankles aligned under me. I noticed I
was shaking. It felt like my bones might give, like the core of
them might just crumble out and leave me brittle and frail.

Then someone touched my shoulder. The boy next to
me. He was looking at the girl beside him, the very last of us
in line, and she was looking back at the door. Which had
opened.

The girl at the end moved quick. She put herself directly
between our captors and that opened door, shielding us
instead of them. The boy next to me got through the door.
I got through. The woman behind me shoved through and
ran into the hallways of the house. There were shouts
from outside.

I turned back to the door as soon as I made it inside,
but no one else came in.

VIOLET

I am not brave by nature. After I opened the door I ducked back from the terrible noise of the bullets and the terror of exposing myself. My limbs froze up against my wishes and it took me several breaths to will myself to step into the doorway again.

The moment my body obeyed, it was pushed back. My cowardice was rewarded by my being knocked beyond the door frame and, as I recovered my balance, by seeing Ellie darting through to safety, and almost giving it up as she immediately turned back again.

ELLIE

The girl's name was Simone, according to the newspapers. I remembered her face so well, even though I'd barely given her more than one grateful glance. Even though I never saw her again.

A bullet glanced off the door frame as I turned, sending a shock of splinters out like little needles into my forearm.

Hands pulled at me, wrapped round me. I recognised her smell. Oranges and soap. Violet.

VIOLET

'Don't you dare.' My hands held her at her upper arm and her waist. I pressed my face against the flat of her shoulder, and I remember I smiled and hurt at the same time. My teeth were so tight against each other my words had to force themselves out. 'Remember, you have to stay alive.' I would remind her over and over if I had to.

'What's going on? What's happening?'

I didn't care who or what they were, but if the men outside were writing the end of all our stories, then I wanted to know what it would say.

ELLIE

I was glad to be interrupted before I had a chance to answer.

'Tell us when we're not by an open door.' March was there. He'd been standing far enough back in the darkness for me not to see him, but he spoke as I turned to answer Violet and to return a little of her tight embrace.

'We can't stay here. Come on.'

We made it back through the corridor before I was able to string things together. My hearing misplaced sources all the time, and my head was ringing with gunshots, but I was almost sure of one thing.

'They were shooting from overhead too. Someone – at least one of them's still inside.'

March slowed and turned back to me just long enough to crash into a shadowed figure leaving one of the rooms along the hall.

TWENTY-SIX

PEACHES

We spent a long time pressed like pinned butterflies to the
wall of the room we'd tumbled into. It's not fear of the
unknown that freezes you. It's knowing exactly what *could*
be waiting, and having to face it anyway, because the
alternative is staying in a room so close to people having an
actual, what-the-fuck *shoot-out* that you feel like you should
be making them refreshments for when they decide to take a
mid-mass-murdering break.

We were standing out of sight on the left side of the
door. The hallway beyond was dark – everything was dark
now for some reason, though a little light made it in through
the broken window. Blue from the police cars. I watched
Joe's jaw clench, and felt his hand tighten round mine at
the same time. Decision made. One good thing about
running for our lives: it meant he hadn't given up on his. For
a while back there I'd thought Sam and Doug would take
him with them.

He glanced at me. I nodded.

We ran through the door together.

But it was only Joe that somehow came out the other side in a flailing struggle with a man clad entirely in black.

JOE

'GET THE FUCK OFF ME! GET THE FUCK OFF!'

Even now I can hear how loud and stupid I sounded, screaming in his face like that. *Screaming*, after an hour of whispers and sneaking from room to room. It was just . . . panic. I go back over it now and it's crazy, but I don't know that I could have reacted any other way.

VIOLET

March wasn't fighting back. He was fighting to get away from an attacker so confused that he seemed to be pulling him in with one hand and fighting him off with the other. I tried to press myself into the space between them, using my hands to prise them apart. 'March! March!'

PEACHES

'*March?*' Joe and whoever he was fighting blended together in the darkness. I had to duck in close to be able to make either of them out. There were two others – the girl who'd shouted looked like Violet Chikezie, quietest girl in class, now almost growling at Joe as she pushed him back. There was Ellie Kimber again somehow, standing to the side, looking shell-shocked.

And there was March. Last seen applying the theory of retro computer games to the art of staying alive. It looked like it was still working for him, only now he'd switched cartridges to *Streetfighter*. 'March!'

I'd been sure he must have died for me. Or instead of me. I'd been certain he'd given up his chance of survival just to lend me an extra life. Since those two slow seconds it had taken me to remember his name, I'd had it circling in my head, guilty and grateful.

I don't know who was more surprised when I pushed past Violet to wrap my arms around him.

ELLIE

'Joe?'

For all the noise – the shouting, the gunfire that seemed to echo into the hallways from every direction now, the panic and the scuffle – I couldn't seem to get my voice above a whisper.

He was alive. Somehow.

But he looked at me, and I could see the two empty spaces that walked beside him. I think that I saw something emptier in his eyes.

He was breathing hard, and just nodded at me. It was an answer to three questions at once.

247

PEACHES

I felt March startle as I hugged him. It took a good thirty seconds of telling him how glad I was that he was alive before his arms figured out an appropriate response and wrapped tight round my waist.

'One side of the stage collapsed,' he told me, and I could feel him calming since no more punches were being thrown his way. 'Most of us were able to run for it then.'

'You cleared the Tetris board,' I tried.

'And was given a bunch of extra lives, Alhamdulillah.' He gave a shaky breath that sounded like an attempt at a laugh. 'It's felt like that all night.'

'Well, let's hope we've all got a few left.' I smiled, pulling back finally to check on Joe.

He'd calmed down, too.

Ellie Kimber was holding both his hands in hers.

VIOLET

It was strange, but in that moment I almost felt safe. Safety is such a relative term, it changes meaning depending on the situation. A man balanced on a small plank above a piranha-filled river may feel safe because he is not in the water. This was the small, safe space in which we stood. Danger on many sides, perhaps on all of them. But we were balanced somewhere just out of its reach.

Joe's shouting had not attracted attention. The focus

of the men who had been so intent on killing us had been pulled away by the prospect of killing or being killed by those outside.

That didn't feel good. I don't imagine the man standing on the plank would feel *good*, either. But it felt safer than the alternative.

I allowed myself to think again about surviving. About whether my family were behind the police lines, safe but just beyond my reach. I felt that they must be, as strongly as at other times during the night I had felt that they must both be dead.

My own momentary sensation of safety gave me the chance to hope for others. But we could not stay where we were.

The girl who had swept March up pulled away from him. Peaches Britten – in my year, like March. We had fewer classes together but I knew her. People had made cruel comments about her sometimes. I had heard her make cruel comments, too, but the nature of defending yourself can sometimes be to fire back.

'Should we leave now?' I asked, gesturing down the turn in the hallway that would take us back the way we had come. Then there would only be a few upturned pieces of furniture to move before we'd be free. There was even the front door, though it felt harder to imagine walking out quite so brazenly through there. But the night still rattled with gunfire.

The sound echoed and was hard to trace. 'Are they shooting down that side as well?'

ELLIE

The question silenced us all for a second. Joe let go of my hands and closed his eyes, as though he'd hear better in isolation.

It was useless. The sound was all one-sided to me anyway, but no one knows better than me the way the mind plays tricks. We all have selective hearing. Our brains impose their own interpretation on the world and nobody wanted to claim they were certain of something and then walk into a trap.

March shook his head. 'Impossible to tell. But if they're all outside now we should go back up –'

JOE

'There's one on the roof,' I put in quickly. Tried not to flinch when March looked at me. 'At least. Could be more we don't know about. Whatever we decide, we're guessing blind.'

PEACHES

March nodded slowly. 'No change there.'

He didn't look away from Joe until Joe ducked his head

and nodded, scrubbing awkwardly with one hand at the back of his neck in what I was learning was a nervous gesture. 'Yeah, and speaking of blind, mate. In the dark . . .'

'In the dark, and with my skin being darker than yours . . .' March filled in. He sounded blunt but not unkind. 'I understand. I watch the news, too. I know what people will look at me and expect.'

Joe didn't look up.

'Is it "the unexpected"?' I asked, tugging at March's sleeve and leading the way along the hall a few steps. Even without knowing where we were going, we had to go *somewhere*. 'Expect the unexpected? Because that would be a great catchphrase. Look, you saved my life, I'm willing to vouch for you not being a terrorist to whoever asks me, but if we could get a little further away from the people who definitely actually are, that would be great.'

ELLIE

'One floor up.' Violet made the decision for all of us. 'We'll go to the second floor, to the room closest to the left stair. From there we'll have two possible exits.'

She phrased so many of her ideas as suggestions. This was firm. No one disagreed.

Joe fell into step beside her, the tension of a moment before wiped out by Violet's confidence and Peaches' humour. 'Sounds good. I'm done with dead ends.'

PEACHES

Ellie looked at me as we followed Violet up the stairs. She leant across. 'You're the one who started that campaign to sing *Hamilton* at the senior concert series, right?'

I wouldn't have been surprised at her knowing my face. Even my name. But I was surprised she knew that. I nodded, and she smiled.

'Thought so. I went every night.'

Then she caught up with Violet, leaving me blinking in her wake.

At the top, Joe was waiting. He slipped his hand back into mine.

JOE

I just felt steadier with her. It was better now we were working as a group, too. Realistically we'd still have had the same chance of survival if we'd run into the wrong person in the dark, but it didn't feel that way. Five against one started feeling like decent odds.

But chances can always be improved. 'What if we find something to arm ourselves with, rather than just wait?'

'Like what?' Peaches shot a look at me, eyebrow raised. 'It's all household stuff up here, and fancy antiques. I mean, I guess we could try fighting them off with a tapestry of a unicorn dancing with a bear – if nothing else, we'd have the element of surprise.'

ELLIE

'It's not such a bad idea,' March said from just behind my shoulder. He was the central dot in the formation we were walking in, two and one and two, like the five on a dice.

I tipped my head back to look at him.

'Surprising them, I mean. Arming ourselves. Not so much the dancing-unicorn thing,' he explained.

I'd knelt outside while bullets skimmed inches above my head. I couldn't imagine anything we found helping us fight back against that. But it meant doing something and doing something felt better than doing nothing.

'We'll see what's in the room we end up in,' I said.

'This one,' Violet said, bringing us all to a stop.

TWENTY-SEVEN

PEACHES

Out of the five of us not a single one still had their phone, although apparently Ellie's had survived the longest. Of course. Who else would remain serene enough during a shooting to avoid the regular pitfalls like falling in a river and commando-crawling practically naked through the mud?

Although she was scuffed and bloody like the rest of us, she was as flawless as always. And you know what? I didn't care. She was as scared as anyone, and she'd found someone else's dropped iPhone as we searched the room.

Which, unfortunately, was as helpful as a brick, when it came to what we could use it for.

'I know it's supposed to be "Historic Hearne House", but do they *need* to be in the technological dark ages to feel authentic?'

VIOLET

'I'm sure they'll have an internet connection, just via cable.'

And not in the room we were in: the flocked parlour. The wallpaper here was deep red and soft to the touch, as if it was made of strips of velvet. It felt like being inside one of the chambers of the heart.

Peaches was trying to get a 4G signal, to find out what the outside world could tell us about what was happening. Standing on the back of an armchair in one corner of the room, the phone raised high above her head, she thought she was close. Ellie and I stood on either side, our hands ringed around her waist for balance.

Then she swore and stepped down on to the seat. 'It's no good. Loading forever. And I can see the shooting from up there.'

The window offered views from one corner of the house. There was nothing directly below it but a gradually spreading ring of police. From here it felt as though we could abseil down somehow and run to them easily, but then, just to the periphery, we'd catch the occasional burst of brightness timed with another short round of gunfire.

Ellie wouldn't get close to the glass. She wouldn't look out at all. I wondered if she was thinking how easily she might still be out there. I kept thinking about that, too.

I sat on the arm of the chair beside Peaches.

Ellie leant in behind me. 'I doubt that the news could tell us much more than we know.'

'It might,' Peaches protested. 'There must be a live blog on one of the news sites by now. Maybe they know who's doing this, and why. Or what they're *doing about it* out there.'

'The press can't get closer than the police, can they?' Ellie added. 'Anyway, there won't be specifics. Not until people's families have been told.'

For the space of a breath we were all silent.

I looked at the phone pinched between Peaches' fingertips, with a battery that wouldn't last much longer. 'But you could call yours. Are they here?'

PEACHES

I shook my head. 'There's only Mum, and she stayed home so she wouldn't miss the live episode of her soap. I may as well not spoil it for her now.'

Mum wouldn't have been watching the news. The one time the TV goes off at our house is when something inescapably awful happens and there's real life on every channel. She's just always been better at keeping up with fictional worlds than the real one. I like fiction too – plays and musicals more than television – but I've never got as close as she does to completely checking out of my own existence in favour of something that's just a story. I've always known it was an escape for her. I just didn't know how to deal with losing her to it.

Now I think I get it. Maybe when you've seen the worst parts of the real world, you don't want to risk wandering into them again, even if it means missing out on the best parts, too. And Mum saw some pretty bad things, before Dad went.

Anyway, I couldn't imagine scaring her over the phone. Or having her not understand me, and not be scared enough.

'I just thought we could leave some poignant messages on Facebook. They'd look great in tomorrow's headlines.'

ELLIE

It was her way of trying to keep hold of herself through the shock. Peaches smothered her fears using humour the way I tried to force mine down through strength of will. I think it must be part of the human condition to hide our truths. There we were, all lying to each other in order to maintain the lies we were telling ourselves to keep from falling apart.

She meant it as a joke, though it made me pause. I hadn't let myself think that far ahead. Now I was. 'That's going to happen, isn't it? They'll put pictures of all of us on the news. Probably the worst things we're tagged in.'

'I don't have a Facebook,' Violet said, then smiled fiercely. 'If they ask, my mother will give them the photo she shows everyone when they ask about me. She paid for it to be taken in a studio in the shopping centre and spent four hours that morning braiding my hair into rows. She likes to say how put together I look. I was nine.'

257

We laughed. For that one moment laughing seemed easy again.

'Maybe I should have filmed some of it,' I said, regretting almost immediately the cooler thought that swallowed some of the warmth. How would we ever explain the horror without videos? But how could video even be enough to describe it?

'Someone will have,' Peaches said. 'Someone's always filming. It didn't have to be you.'

'Did I tell you my dad called?' I said.

VIOLET

Ellie's father had reached her while she was hiding, alone. It was the first time she'd had a chance to tell me exactly what had happened. Since then she had texted him and her mother back to say she was alive, and that they shouldn't call.

She knew he was safe and didn't want to talk to him again until she could say the same for herself. Love makes us into protectors, in whatever way we can be.

There had been no word from my mother. I called and left a new message for her on our borrowed phone.

Out on the hill, police were telling the crowds gathering to turn off their phones for now. Parents were being asked not to call their children, because a ringtone or green light might give away a hiding place. If I'd known that, I might have felt better.

But all I knew was that the world had changed so much, and the time it had taken felt both so short and so long at once, and I hadn't spoken to my mother since the beginning of the end of it.

JOE

'Joe?' Peaches called across to us. March was on his knees next to me, holding an antique table steady on its back while I tried to wrench a leg off. 'Do you want to make a call?'

I shook my head. I could still remember Sam's sister screaming. I had two sisters halfway across the country, living with Mum. And I had Dad. Who'd started the evening in the pub and for all I knew was still there.

Like always, I'd decided I wasn't going to tell him anything until I could tell him something to be proud of.

'March?' Peaches asked.

He shook his head. I watched his hands tighten momentarily around the table edge. I was still dragging uselessly on the leg. I nodded at it. 'Do you want to give me a hand with this?'

Together, we put a foot each on the flat underside of the table, both of us gripping the leg to work it out of its joint.

'Don't want to worry anyone?' I asked after a minute, keeping my voice low enough that it was just between us. He looked across at me, his jaw tight with effort of levering ancient oak out of where it had been successfully stuck for centuries.

'Everyone I know is fine,' he said.

'Parents aren't here?'

For a moment he stopped pulling with me. I almost dragged the table over on top of both of us, stamping my foot down to hold it just in time.

'They work in the city, at the hospital,' he said. I'd looked away, swearing at the splinters in my hands, but I could feel him studying the side of my face. Like maybe I was just making an effort because of jumping him earlier. I questioned myself on that, but I don't think I was. There was something he was keeping back. 'They'll both be busy tonight.'

Understatement, I was guessing. Amberside didn't have a hospital, so all the casualties from here would have to be taken out of town.

'One of my sisters wants to be a nurse,' I said. 'Thinks she can fix everything. She'll kill me for not letting her in on this.'

I kidded myself my sisters would just be pissed off that I didn't keep them up to date with the drama. And that they'd miss whatever small bit of fame for knowing someone caught up in a news story might give them. The whole my-brother-was-there thing making celebrities of them at their universities.

Though they got that afterwards anyway. Except both

of them left uni to stay with me and Dad and didn't go back until the survivors were old news. Turned out, it was just me they cared about.

I was shit not to have appreciated that. But I knew there would be fuss, and nothing good I could tell them while we were still trapped. Why let them know I was alive when that could change any minute? False hope's worse than fear, sometimes.

'My sister is fierce, too.' March's smile was sharp when he spoke about her. 'After we came here, people teased me about my accent, so I stayed silent until I'd got rid of it. Imani just spoke louder. That thing English people do in foreign restaurants? She would do it back, make her words long and slow, as though the person she was speaking to might be too stupid to understand. The one time I was bullied, followed home, Imani was the one to meet them. I was hiding in my room. I don't know what happened, but those lads never troubled me again. Sisters. They would protect you from anything, if they could.'

He rubbed a hand across his chest, the torn pocket of his shirt, then went back to helping me.

I didn't ask where Imani was that night. Didn't have a chance to.

The table leg squealed and cracked as it finally came free in our hands.

ELLIE

March came over to show off a thick wooden club with jagged edges.

'Well, I'm intimidated, at least,' Peaches said. 'Though it's sort of the opposite of bringing a gun to a knife fight.'

It had been quiet for a few minutes by then. None of us liked the quiet any more, all it meant was uncertainty. Peaches climbed off the chair and went to press her face to the window. I caught myself shivering. Violet caught me too, I think. She rested a hand on my arm.

'No rusty nails?' I asked, looking at the table leg.

Joe followed March across. 'I don't think the Tudors used nails, did they?'

We all looked at Violet.

She shrugged. 'I don't know *everything*.'

VIOLET

It was still quiet outside. Every time it got that way my thoughts strayed back to my mother and how much time I was wasting when I could be finding her. The line of police looked so close from up here. If we could just make it to them, we would be safe.

I said, 'Every time I ask myself if it might be over, it seems to turn into the beginning of something new.'

Joe nodded. He was starting to say something when Peaches spoke over him from the window.

262

'There's something new happening now. Has someone got away from them? Two of them! They're running away from the house. The police . . . the police are backing away . . .'

She frowned, confused. 'No, hold on. It's not an escape. It's one of them. Right underneath us. He's pulling a girl with him, running right for the police. They're going to shoot them both – they're . . .'

The light outside grew brilliant for one shining second, before the window she was standing by blew inward in a hail of projectiles.

TWENTY-EIGHT

When the work phone rings after seven p.m., I always know
what it's going to be. We don't have off-hours in this role
and the work we do is intense. Sometimes it's a lad on a
bridge, sometimes a domestic turned particularly nasty. There
have been more than a few nights where my training's been
tested to its limit.

Nothing like this.

Working for a regional unit, very much out of the way
as far as head office is concerned, I never expected to deal
with a terrorist incident of this scale. We've had a couple of
young boys around here getting big ideas from the internet
and getting in over their heads, that's been the worst of it.

So when the call came, when they gave me the details: a
concert, gunmen, a crowd full of schoolchildren, I could feel
myself looking for a reason not to attend.

Well, I'm a mother. Two little ones. The *thought* of
children being slaughtered like that gripped at my very soul.

And then I shook myself off, got dressed and got down there. Of course I did. Well, I'm a mother.

One of the instigators had provided a phone number for us early in the evening, approximately correlating with their entry into the house. Called it in, said they'd talk when they were ready. They said *we* should be ready, and then they cut the call off. Turned the phone off, too. We kept trying that number while officers cleared the field – all the ones still able to walk themselves out of it – and we got into position.

You have to be calm, doing what I do. I'm often told it's like a superpower, the way I stay dead calm no matter what. You raise your voice, you let a note of panic creep in, you let them think you don't know what you're doing, you've had it. But that night I could feel my heart hammering in my chest like it never has before. Every time I spoke my throat felt so tight I wasn't sure the words would make it through. And that was before the call finally connected.

He was already speaking when it was passed to me.

'–re ready to talk.'

I took a breath, my mind crowding with the usual strategics. Thank him for speaking with me. Establish a connection. Facilitate an exchange. Listen to his demands. Be a sounding board for the irrational. Be understanding of the incomprehensible. Give him options that aren't the worst-case scenario.

He hung up before I could part my lips.

But that isn't unusual. It can take time to forge the trust needed for somebody to start talking. In situations where the hostage takers are rational enough to know they're looking at a loss of life or freedom, whatever the outcome, it's going be slow to achieve a good result. A marathon, not a sprint.

You just have to hope they don't outrun you.

In this case they were endlessly a few lengths ahead. We weren't prepared for them to exit the building with hostages and no warning. I look back on whether we should have been, *could* have been, but if there was any rule book for the way these scenarios play out it wouldn't be in there.

Hearne House has written its own chapter in the rule books now.

Someone thrust a loudhailer into my hands. I got out a few words, barely audible over the firearms officers yelling warnings. And utterly pointless. All officers without shields were pulled back as they started firing on us. From behind the wheels of a parked van I watched as those men dragged young kids up in front of them, daring us to shoot. Making us the murderers.

There was no space for me, no space for negotiation amid all the escalation. And, well, we know where that ended. I'll never forget seeing . . . I'll never forget.

I haven't reconsidered my career path in a long time. It's draining work: you take on the emotions and desires of the kind of people we're not supposed to understand. But the success rate is good, and when we're successful those are real lives I'm saving.

Just not that night. They never gave me the chance.

They never gave anyone a chance.

• • • • • • • • • • •

TWENTY-NINE

PEACHES

The first thing I heard was my name. Joe was *screaming* it.

VIOLET

Ellie had hold of his arms, wrestling with him. 'Don't take it out. Don't touch her, you'll make it worse.'

PEACHES

I could hear Ellie's voice through a weird metallic howl, like someone was whipping a wire through the air above my head. My vision was full of sparks.

ELLIE

'*Joe*, it looks worse than it is. Just don't touch her.' I hoped I was right. I thought I was.

He ripped himself out of the hold I had on him.

JOE

There was no way I wasn't going to touch her. March was already crouching down next to her when I knelt down in the shattered glass. My knees were wrecked anyway. There was a small, painful reminder that I'd torn them up already when we climbed in through the window, but the ache meant nothing to me.

VIOLET

'Be careful,' March murmured. He put his hands over the shard of glass that stuck out from Peaches' ribcage like a silver dagger, just in case Joe made a grab for it.

PEACHES

I tried to open my eyes again. It was easier this time. The dizziness was receding slowly, like a wave that had come close to drowning me before the tide ebbed back out. The shapes above me clarified themselves into March, and Ellie and Violet, and Joe.

'My head is *killing* me.'

JOE

I laughed. It was just tension finding the quickest exit valve. Relief felt too premature, but hearing her voice punched all the breath I'd been holding out of my lungs, and I had to struggle to find my own. 'Yeah? I think you took a bit of a knock.'

I cradled her head in my hands, brushing my fingers through her hair, beyond grateful that at least there was no damage there. Just scratches all across her skin. Face, arms, everything that was exposed.

The place where the window had exploded into her wasn't even bleeding. She tried to move. 'Don't sit up.'

PEACHES

I took a shallow breath and screwed my eyes up again against the tears that stung them.

'Joe, I think a person just blew up outside. I need to check what's going on.'

The bang hadn't knocked out my memory, even if I'd lost consciousness for a minute after hitting the ground. I could remember everything I'd seen, even that split-second switch between expecting to see someone crumple to the ground and watching them thrown up in the air, instead.

The explosion hadn't hit the house with too much force, just enough to throw me back and shatter a couple more of the windows that weren't already broken. The *boom* is a sound I'll replay over and over.

VIOLET

'I'll look. I can tell you what I see.'

Ellie murmured my name softly, as if it was a warning. '*Violet.*'

'I won't get too close. We have to know.'

ELLIE

I balled my hands into fists at my side and nodded.

Violet stood back from the window and to one side, the same angle Peaches had been at when she'd mentioned being able to watch the gunfire. I counted my breaths.

'There are people on the ground. The police are pulling them back, dragging them. I think they're police, too.'

One officer was killed in this part of the operation, I know now. Five injured.

'Can you see the bomber?'

'No. There's someone – but she's not one of them. She's wearing white.'

Angelique, the girl brought across as a shield. Thrown clear of the blast. A miraculous survival. Seventy percent burns.

'But it was a bomb. Or a grenade, or something.' I'd bitten down so hard on my lip the corner of it was ragged and copper-tasting. 'They have bombs now.'

'No,' Violet said, and she looked at me. 'They *are* bombs.'

VIOLET

If we had run, it would have been towards that line of police and the illusion of safety behind it. There were parents and people from the town too, ignoring advice to try and help. I will never forget that there are people in this world who walked into hell by choice, to free those of us who had been trapped there.

I narrowed my eyes and watched for some time, but I could not see the man who had carried the explosion strapped to his chest.

Of course, I know now. There was very little left of him to see.

ELLIE

Things happened quickly after that. There was another burst of light, this one blinding. Another bang, much louder than the first, and when our senses started to recover from the double impact, Violet shouted that the police were running towards the house.

'Was that the second shooter, is he gone?' My voice was louder than I meant, both my hearing and non-hearing ear ringing.

'I don't know . . . They have their weapons raised.'

'It was a flashbang,' Joe said, still on his knees but every muscle tensed. 'It's a thing the police use to disorient people. They're coming in.'

JOE

Peaches used my distraction to prop herself up enough to see the fragment of glass sticking out of her front. She gripped my wrist viciously hard.

'Don't move,' March reminded her, before I could.

The spike was about the same size as her palm, when she held her hand up against it. I didn't know how much more of it there might be, buried inside. I just thought that if she was OK now then I'd do everything to keep her that way. If she moved, it could dig somewhere it hadn't reached yet. Slice through something important. I don't know much biology, but I know where we keep our most necessary parts.

PEACHES

'It just feels like I've been punched.' A dull feeling, not sharp. The vicious spike sticking out of me didn't seem to match up with it.

I didn't feel mortally wounded. I was more interested in what was happening outside the house than inside me. Violet's halting reports weren't enough. Would we be safe now? Would the police reach us? Should we wait, or should we run? Was this over, or were they chasing a human bomb up the stairs in our direction?

'Joe, help me. I've got to get up.'

VIOLET

'No,' Joe whispered like a reflex, before the rattle of another round of shots cut through the quiet.

'Where are they firing from?' Ellie was at my side in the space of a breath, her face turned away from the window, towards the door.

March stood, his head tipped back. 'That's above us.'

One round exhausted itself and a new barrage began. 'Those are below.'

ELLIE

Downstairs, the one-sided shooting had turned into a two-way battle. I tried not to think about what that meant for everyone who'd been marched outside with me and hadn't made it back in.

PEACHES

I struggled against Joe's hands on my shoulder, managing to push an elbow back to support myself. The noise from above us had stopped now, which only meant that we didn't know where it would move to next. 'I have to – I can't just lay here.'

JOE

'OK.' I tried to keep my breath steady. Tried to steady my voice. The glass shard was almost invisible in the dark, but I kept an eye on where I knew it was as I wrapped an arm round her shoulders. I willed it not to move. 'OK. I've got you.'

PEACHES

I pushed myself up a little further, and that's when the pain got sharp.

ELLIE

'Table leg?' I looked around for the makeshift weapon, the only one we'd found.

March was retrieving it from the side of the armchair. He swung it out like a baseball bat. 'Just in case.'

VIOLET

Just in case, I picked up a paperweight from the writing desk against the wall. Pulling at the gold stem of the lamp there revealed it would be too heavy for any of us to carry.

ELLIE

The shooting was still going on. Still below us, for now.

JOE

Peaches was breathing fast, pain announcing itself as a whimper on every exhale. I tried to lay her back down, reweighing the risk between moving and not moving for the thousandth time, but she shook her head. 'Please.'

PEACHES

Getting on to my knees felt like climbing Everest. But I got there.

VIOLET

Joe helped Peaches up with his hands at her back. I held mine out for her to take.

ELLIE

The floor shook underneath us.

VIOLET

Another explosion. We felt the impact more, because it was inside the house. Below us. Plaster from the ceiling dislodged in flakes and fluttered down around us. It was like being trapped inside a snow globe.

'Flashbang?' March asked Joe.

JOE

'Or we're down to one,' I said.

Peaches was on her feet now, taking small steps. I took her arm from Violet.

PEACHES

The silence stretched out for a thousand years. It was probably thirty seconds in non-terrified time.

VIOLET

Then we heard running along the corridor above our heads. It didn't sound like heavy boots, but what way was there to know?

Running, down the stairway to the left of us.

I was at the door, the paperweight heavy in my hand, Ellie's fingertips hooked into mine on the other side.

ELLIE

'Don't.' I could only whisper it.

'They might need help.' March was behind me, then moving past.

'We have to see.' Violet stepped out too, both of them, into the dark hallway.

JOE

We got across to the door. I didn't know how well Peaches would be able to run, but if we had to, we had to.

PEACHES

Whatever it took.

VIOLET

It wasn't one of them. I knew that. I knew from the weight of their footfalls, I knew from a feeling in my chest. It wasn't one of them. The hall was so dark, I wished that I'd never thought to cut the light. They were almost at the point where the stairway met the hall where we stood.

PEACHES

'Are you ready?' Joe murmured somewhere near my ear.

What a stupid question.

VIOLET

They were so close.

ELLIE

It was so dark.

VIOLET

It was impossible to make out who it was, the slight form that made it to the bottom of the stairway, almost into the hall. But I knew her voice.

Miss Ewell screamed, 'Go,' to us, as the air around her was peppered with bullets.

THIRTY

VIOLET

'Run,' Ellie said beside me, and my body struggled to translate the word into movement.

Our teacher was dead on the stairs. Who knew what was coming behind her? Who knew what might be ahead of us?

Run.

'Which way?' I heard myself sobbing. 'Which way?'

ELLIE

Run. All my life I've been running as though someone else's life depended on it. Now maybe it did.

'With me,' I whispered to Violet, linking my arm with hers.

PEACHES

Ellie and Violet took off ahead of us, shoeless and silent down the hall. Reflex pulled me after them, held back for half a second by Joe's grip on my arm.

JOE

March was just standing there, holding that bloody table leg like he was going to be our last line of defence.

PEACHES

'Come on. You're with us,' Joe told him, and we ran linked like a daisy chain.

I tried not to lag too much. The pain was easy not to think about, because everything hurt by then. I could have traced a pull or a twist or an ache to every single limb. The stabbing in my chest was just one more twinge, but my breath was running short.

We were already a few steps behind the other two, trying to keep up.

VIOLET

We ran towards the central staircase and its three choices: up, down or along the hall.

ELLIE

There were other noises in the hallways. Things that could have been footsteps above us and below. In other corridors. Maybe on the stairs. Doors banging. The confusion of similar sounds was disorienting. I couldn't focus, so I did what I always do when I run, I retreated into my head and found the rhythm there. *London Bridge is falling down, falling down.*

JOE

'I think there's someone coming up,' March said, half under his breath.

PEACHES

I could hear it: heavy steps. But there were sounds coming from the hall above us, too. Not from behind us yet, though I expected to be followed so much that my shoulders were braced, ready for the hit. But I wasn't just going to wait for a bullet to take me.

JOE

'I think there's someone coming up,' March called, louder, as Ellie hit the central staircase and turned downward. Violet heard him and kept running straight on.

VIOLET

My hand caught on hers. She looked up at me.

ELLIE

And when I looked down again, he was there. With his blue
eyes. Even in the dark they were so blue.

PEACHES

Too late to stop, we crashed into the landing behind her.
March – it was March who started up the stairs. He pulled
Joe after him. Joe pulled me. I held out my hand towards
Ellie and Violet.

VIOLET

'*ELLIE!*'

JOE

And then there were no stairs below us. No Ellie. No
anything, except the darkness, the receding explosion, and
Violet's long scream.

PEACHES

The world lurched under me, and then half of it wasn't there
any more. The step under me crumbled. Joe dragged me up
on to something more solid and I fell to my knees coughing

out dust and ash. There was no time. I was choking on the debris of a human bomb and there was no time.

JOE

We half carried her, half dragged her up the rest of that flight of stairs, me and March, and at the top she got to her feet again. I don't know how.

PEACHES

What else could I do? I still had feet. My face felt scorched and my lungs were shrivelling inside me and I didn't know if the stabbing feeling in my chest was the glass or grief, and I wanted to scream until my throat dried out but there wasn't time. I still had feet. So I used them.

VIOLET

I flew and I fell and there was no time for me to separate the sensations. The stair I had been standing on gave way and I landed with the rubble and broken struts of wood that had blown out of it. The impact jarred every bone. I heard myself clatter inside.

PEACHES

There was no rhyme or reason to the direction we picked. Decisions taken then weren't the end result of a process of thought. They were a roll of the dice. All that mattered was to run. Run while we still could.

JOE

I think we knew, after we lost Ellie. I think all three of us were waiting for it. Our turn.

PEACHES

He was waiting for us at the end of the hall.

JOE

He had his arm raised. Holding a pistol. A handgun, not one of the hunting rifles I'd seen them with in the grounds.

PEACHES

You think things like that happen in slow motion.

JOE

In the films it's always in slow motion.

285

PEACHES

But in the films dead people look just like they're sleeping, and people who've been shot tumble to the ground, dead in one strike.

JOE

It was quicker than I could have believed. I didn't even see his finger hit the trigger. Didn't hear the bang of it until after.

PEACHES

But you have slow-motion memories of being shot, because the moment it happens is *so fast* that your mind has to replay it afterwards, while it's trying to process what just happened.

I moved. He shot me.

Or: he shot. I moved.

JOE

The bullet was meant for March. I don't know how she was so quick.

PEACHES

Three times lucky. I'd seen March move first. He raised his arm, the only one of us with anything vaguely resembling a weapon, pointless as it was, and something in me knew the first shot would be for him. I couldn't let that happen.

Three times I'd been lucky. The fourth's the charm.

JOE

He shot again. Barely flinched after the first, then sent a pellet of nothing following it. The gun jammed, or the gun was empty. I didn't know, didn't care, barely noticed as he turned and ran.

She was still just standing there.

PEACHES

And I thought . . . *Wow, that thing about people not immediately tumbling over when they're shot is really true.*

And I thought, *I've been shot. I've been* shot. And I looked down.

And Joe and March were there to catch me when I fell.

JOE

March was crying. It happened all of a sudden, like someone had flicked a switch in him. He was crying over her. He was looking at me and saying, 'What do we do?', and I was saying, 'Please, please.'

PEACHES

There were words around me, begging me for something.
There was a world around me, but I sunk into my own head,
my own world. I was still thinking, which seemed like a good
sign. I was thinking how I was sixteen. And I was thinking
how sixteen's *nothing*. I didn't feel old enough to die.
I hadn't put in any preparation.

JOE

She moved her hand slowly across her ribs to where the
blood was starting to flow.

PEACHES

And I thought, *I guess it doesn't matter about the glass shard
now.*

VIOLET

I crawled over the dirt and rubble until I found her.
Everything was hard and sharp, and I felt hard and sharp
inside. I found her by touch, the darkness resolving slowly
into just enough light to make out that my right hand was on
her hip. That my left hand was on her leg. That legs should
not twist that way.

I ran my hand up to where her arm was thrown across

her chest. Her skin was still so warm, or maybe mine was so cold. Her sequinned dress was fused to her like mermaid scales, tiny sparks of light still somehow caught in them. Trying not to touch the places where her clothes were melted into her skin, I found her shoulder, and I laid myself down beside her, my body stretched out alongside hers like a mirror image. Her face shone under whatever dim light there was to catch. The burn had bitten down to white bone on her cheek, and her skin gleamed wetly elsewhere. I wanted to take her face in my hands, to press my mouth against her cheek.

'You're so beautiful.' My eyes stung with tears. I told her again and again, 'You are so beautiful.'

JOE

We'd lifted Peaches between us when we heard shots again. They were close, but the hallway was clear and my legs were too heavy to run any further. We took her just across the hall, closing the door to one of the bedrooms as we got inside. The room was a mess, things knocked everywhere. We weren't the first to pick it. Bullet holes scarred the wall like pockmarks.

March pulled the sheets off the bed and spread them on the floor beside it, as hidden from the door as we could get her. I laid Peaches down while he grabbed a pillow to go under her head.

The gunshots were like drumbeats. I listened for the

little voice in my head that had told me to survive, just stay alive, and then told me when I might as well give up. It wasn't there. I found her voice instead, telling me not to be such a fucking idiot. Telling me not to waste the time I had left. Whatever time I had left.

March moved to the door. The drumming was getting close now, persistently on the periphery of my thoughts. And then it stopped.

I could still hear their feet. Coming close. Right outside.

March stood guard, facing it alone.

I brushed her hair back. If you've got seconds left, what do you do so they're not wasted?

I had just seconds left. I moved half a breath before the door was slammed back on its hinges. 'March, no –'

THIRTY-ONE

When I was very young, I slept badly. Every night there was a new nightmare. I don't know why. I was only four, or five, and five-year-olds aren't supposed to have those kind of worries. I must have cried during my sleep, back then, because I remember often being pulled from my bed to find that my mother had heard me through the walls and come in to wake me with a hug. It made me less afraid to sleep the next evening.

That night last October felt, in some moments, like it was never-ending. In other moments it felt like it would end any minute. Either way, the whole time I was sure there would be no waking up safe from that nightmare.

I expected the end to come at last as the door crashed open. As much as death can be called an ending, I felt sure that moment would be mine. So I stood with that table leg laying across my palms, ready to swing if anything came close enough to swing at. I knew the weight of the polished wood was meant to be reassuring, but it just felt like a way to occupy my hands.

I wasn't really waiting to fight. The problem is that I'm

too good at working out the odds, and mine were very unfavourable. I spoke with God inside my head. Recited Allahu Akbar on the whisper of my breath. I was crying too, like I had as a child, but silently. I knew that calling out wouldn't bring anyone to pull me safely away from my fears. I never imagined I could be woken from that nightmare with a hug.

But I was.

The door opened and I heard my name called from behind me. The sound of Joe racing to get close. I threw my arms out to keep him behind me and closed my eyes. *Please*.

I don't know if I meant please save me or please kill me as I faced what would come through that door. Just, please, let the nightmare end.

And somehow it did.

I woke to the sound of men I couldn't see screaming *GET ON YOUR KNEES! GET ON YOUR KNEES!* And to find I couldn't do what they were asking because Joe Mead had wrapped his arms around me, tight. He'd put his hand on the back of my head and cradled it to his shoulder. He'd bent his head against mine.

Mama used to rock me and hush me with songs and lullabies.

We trembled and rocked too, holding on to each other as though we each had our arms locked round the mast of a ship on a storm-wracked ocean.

The room filled out around us. It wasn't death waiting

at the door, but five or six men: armed police, still shouting. They moved around us, hustling to the window and over to the bed we'd laid Peaches next to.

CLEAR.

I remember it in the same hazy way that you can still remember some particular dreams, years after having them. There were hands on my shoulder, on my arms, trying to separate Joe's hold from mine, but neither of us could let go of the other.

I don't think even he knows why he did it. Why that's the last thing that he chose to do. Just like I didn't really know why I was still holding on to that table leg, trying to keep him safe to the last second.

The nightmare ended with a hand smoothing over my shaking shoulders, and a voice saying the same thing Mama always used to. 'It's OK. It's OK now.'

But that was just how I woke up. It didn't shake off the nightmare into something not-real. That night in October has been the longest I've ever lived through. It's still going on for me even now today, as we retread the minutes to see what there might be to learn from them.

We were left with one police officer, while the others moved on to secure the hall. Joe took a breath deep enough to make up for the hundred he'd been holding and broke away from me to begin begging for help for Peaches. The officer knelt down beside her to look at the mess that had been made of her chest and I'm sure that all the right things were said, but I didn't hear them because I was focused on his face. The utter lack of hope there.

Joe wanted to stay. I would have stayed too, but we weren't allowed and we were too done to fight any more with anybody who wasn't actively trying to kill us. We were told that those who could walk had to leave.

Violet was told the same. She said they carried her away from Ellie in the end, because being able to walk and being capable of walking *away* were such different things.

We were shepherded into a line of ash-faced people and led towards the bridge. They told us not to look to the sides as we crossed the field, and not to look down as we walked over the water. 'I don't think they understand what we've already seen,' Joe said to the air in front of him.

I didn't look anywhere other than my feet.

As we made it into the road, the lights of Hearne House flickered back on.

There were people with silver wraps to put round our shoulders, and coaches waiting to take the unharmed among us to the town hall. Joe was hurt, more than he'd realised, with glass in his leg that had worked itself bone-deep, and my parents worked at the hospital, so we were assessed and moved into the line for a different coach. One for the walking wounded.

They left the dead where they'd fallen. The night was clear and bright without the slightest wisp of cloud that might count as a warning for rain, so no one was moved until the next morning. They tented the bodies with sheets. They photographed each one: from a distance and then close enough to show the precise angle of the shot that ended them. There's a folder of all those photographs. A family album of last days.

I listened when the forensic investigators spoke about their examination of the scene. One of them cried: so many teenagers. Just children, really, to her. She had a daughter of her own, and couldn't it have been her daughter as easily as it could have been them?

She said that they were gentle with the people who could no longer feel. They closed eyes, smoothed hair, but didn't move them.

Parents, children, sisters, brothers, friends. Many of their families waited on that road by the bridge all that night and into the next day, when the bodies were finally carried from the field.

If I could have chosen, I would have stayed with them and waited, too.

The coach Joe and I were moved to was silent as it drove. Once or twice someone moaned, or cried out, or I'd hear a sob. Paramedics checked on people, speaking in soft voices. But it's the silence I remember. The kind of silence that feels louder than the noise that came before.

I'd rather have talked. The echoes of gunfire in my head might have been quieter if I'd talked over them. But Joe stared out of the window for most of the drive, and then we were at the hospital in the city and he was pushing up out of his seat, palms flat to the window.

There was a crowd waiting, and one man set apart from them at the front. He was tall, his forearms and throat traced over with the outlines of tattoos, but that wasn't why he stood out. He cried the way I haven't seen many men cry. And I have seen so many men cry now. And he caught sight of Joe's face and started yelling his name, crying harder all the time.

Joe looked out at him as though this was someone it was a struggle to recognise.

It shouldn't have been. They had the same eyes.

In the seat in front of me, a woman stood up to leave the bus, then sat back down immediately, her legs giving way underneath her. I think she was a teacher, but not one I knew. 'Can I help?' I left Joe and walked with her up to the sliding doors of the hospital, bending low enough for my shoulders to be a support for her arm.

Then I went back to the bus. Joe had gone, but there were other people trying to get off, some of them pushing, others afraid and still not believing they were safe. There were only so many people to help. I went back and forward three or four times, walking with people who were unable or scared to walk alone. Then the bus was empty.

It turned round to go back for more. Going on, through the night.

That night is still going on for so many of us.

Violet's little brother, Ade, was found early in the rescue operation, and alive. He went on to survive surgeries to remove the bullets from his shoulder and his leg. I brought him some comics to help him through his time on the ward. No superheroes. A story where ordinary people save the world.

Her mother was brought back from the house a day later. She had been found among the trees with Ade, folded over him, her body his shelter and shield.

Violet's father was taken for respite care after the loss of his wife. Violet spread her time between visiting him and Ade, and the ward attached to the burns unit, one level up, where they were saving what they could of Ellie's skin.

Ellie's parents seemed to be there night and day, even after the first grafts were done and she was allowed to wake from the induced sleep they'd put her in while the pain would have been overwhelming.

And Joe waited for Peaches. By the bedside in her room, with the television constantly on, playing an endless rotation of her mum's favourite programmes.

There are people still in hospital now, and more still making regular visits. Far more of us were referred to counsellors, more counsellors than I would have thought Amberside even had. There are support groups. Not everyone goes.

Then there are those who wait for night-time, when closing their eyes brings everything back, all the little details clearer in their broken memories than they had been even at the time. The things they escaped then still stalk them now.

And there are the people still waiting, though they've been told no one will ever come home.

Eighty-three people died at Hearne House. Seven more in the days after. Dozens more were injured, many badly. There are a lot of people still waiting.

That night, as the bus moved back out of the car park, back to the house on the hill, I was still waiting. Outside the hospital doors, looking in.

That was where my mother found me.

I thought she and my Baba would have been kept too busy on their shifts but of course they weren't. They were waiting, too.

Mama burst through the swing doors as though she'd heard me crying in the next room and pulled me into the kind of hug that had always made the nightmares end. And then she held my shoulders, and she looked at me.

And I told her that my sister, Imani, was fine. She was fine. She was smiling when I kissed her face, before I had to leave her where she was lying to run and hide under the stage. They wouldn't let her come home from Hearne House yet. Not that night. We would just have to wait.

And I pressed a hand to the bullet hole in my shirt.

• • • • • • • • • •

THIRTY-TWO

PEACHES

I died. Actually, I died three times. Because, I guess, something out there has a warped sense of humour. Or maybe just really believes in evening out a debt.

My heart stopped first on the way to the hospital, and then twice more during surgery, where a team of people spent six hours picking bullet fragments out of my insides and trying to sew me back up as fully and functionally as possible. Not that I remember that part, of course. Consciousness came back to me in fits and scraps the first few days, and all I can really recall of it is waking up a few brief times, already feeling too exhausted to do anything but go back to sleep. I dreamed to the beeping of my oxygen monitor woven into the theme tune of all Mum's favourite shows.

She was at the hospital with me every single day through the weeks I was kept in. The TV was on the whole time, but when I did finally wake long enough to look across at her, it was me she was watching.

JOE

All Dad had wanted was to get me home. I didn't know he could be like that with me. So gentle. The way he was when my sisters were little, if one of them got hurt. He'd treat them like they were glass, while I got told to man up and get on with it. When they left with Mum it was like I stopped seeing the kindness in him. He was just the ex-boxer who'd been beaten in all the bouts that really mattered and had given up thinking there was anything worth fighting for.

He told me he loved me enough that night to try to make up for seventeen years. Treated me like glass. The precious kind, not the vicious spikes I'd been grinding to powder inside my knee. It took ages before I saw the doctor about that, and when he said I wouldn't get to see the surgeon until the next day – all the theatres were overbooked twenty times over with cases way more touch and go – I understood, but I cried anyway. In front of my *dad*.

And it was fine.

That was the night I told him I wanted to run, if I still could. If I was good enough, and if my knees weren't fucked. I wanted to do something that mattered. Maybe I was dreaming, but I wanted to break records.

And it was fine.

'That was me, once,' he said. 'But you'll be better.'

I fell asleep against his side in the waiting room after that. Every time I woke I'd drag myself over to the desk to ask about Peaches, and every time I got told they couldn't confirm any names to non-family.

Once, after a new receptionist had come on shift, I thought I saw her flinch at the name. A flicker of recognition. I tried again, 'Peaches. Peaches Britten?' But she shook her head.

Didn't get much sleep after that.

PEACHES

One thing I haven't asked much about is all the time Joe spent sitting beside my mother. Like, I know it was *days*. Days where it was just them, and the soap operas, and Joe's dad apparently coming in every few hours with fresh supplies from the express supermarket across the street. Days of me totally out of it, dreaming and probably drooling on my pillow, but at least not dying.

Three times was enough, when it came to that. I'm not sure if the weird irony involved in surviving as often as I died should make me re-evaluate my theory of invincibility. I mean, does it imply I've used up my luck, or just confirm I'm indestructible?

I've only realised recently how invincible I used to feel before all this happened. I didn't have any reason for it then. But that's how we get through life without becoming nervous wrecks, isn't it? By believing it couldn't happen to us. Things that happen to other people never feel quite real. You're always safe, until you're not.

JOE

I practically moved into Peaches' room. Her mum, Tilda, didn't seem to mind, as long as I didn't talk through anything important on the TV.

They told me she'd died in surgery about three seconds before they told me they got her back, and all I could think was that if I stayed with her all the time from then on I'd never have to live three seconds like that again.

And it was easier for me to be in Peaches' room. Dad knew where I was, and Mum and my sisters came up when they arrived. But hardly anyone else would have thought to look for me there. Mum told me Sam's parents had come to the house. I sort of blanked it out.

For the first day afterwards, while Peaches was in the ICU, before she got moved to her own room, whatever channel you turned the television to, we were the only thing on it.

But only for a day.

That first day there were fuzzy videos taken from Twitter and Snapchat, black rectangles where all you could see were shaky lights in the distance and all you could hear were gunshots and screams. There were photos they'd mined off social media, and slowly growing lists of names.

The next day a holiday company went bust, stranding hundreds of people in Magaluf. And there was a sinkhole in a motorway just outside London, where a Megabus fell part of the way in.

They were just a couple of stories tagged on to the end of the news, which still carried the lists, the photos and the videos I had to mute every bloody time they came on, but it was a relief just to know that the world was still going on outside.

We, and Hearne House, and everything that had happened there, were just a small part of it. Things would move on.

On the fourth day Peaches woke up.

PEACHES

Imagine waking up feeling like some kind of heavy-goods vehicle has broken down on your chest, to find out the prettiest boy in school now knows your mother better than he knows you. I'm still not sure which felt more crushing.

In the muddle of my memory it felt like barely a few hours had passed since I'd felt self-conscious about letting somebody like Joe Mead see my bare arms. When my new reality settled in, I had to consider that now he'd seen me with a chest drain pumping internal unpleasantness out of my deflated lung, and bandages across my upper torso to cover thoracotomy incisions that have left my body looking like a badly made patchwork quilt. Not to mention the likely sleep-drooling.

And still, when I woke up properly, he only looked relieved. I've never seen anyone so pleased to see me.

JOE

I stepped out for a bit. Which was a wrench, but I thought
the first thing she needed was some time with her mum. She'd
been waking up for a couple of minutes here and there, only
semi-conscious, and if that's all this was, I couldn't take those
minutes for myself.

Besides, she's nice, Peaches' mum. Seems like she's away
with the fairies sometimes, or away with whoever's had their
baby stolen by an evil twin on her American soap operas. But
she's there. Sometimes when I stayed later than I meant to,
I'd wake up in the chair by Peaches' bed to find her crying.
She never made a sound.

My mum came in to see us a few times, too. I probably
saw her more those few weeks than in the last year. She's
talking about moving closer. I think I'd like that.

When I finally went back in, Peaches was still awake,
looking confused by the number of people checking machines
and readings around her and hanging a new bag of painkiller
in her drip. 'I always swear by arnica,' Tilda told them. She
ruffled a hand through my hair as she walked past me
through the door. 'Just going to pop to the vending machine.'

Pulse, oxygen, God knows what else got checked off
before we were left alone. It takes a lot of machines to look
after one person. When the last nurse went out, I sat on the
edge of the bed.

'You took your time.'

PEACHES

I sucked in a breath half as deep as I'd have liked to have
been able to. I still felt like I'd just run a marathon with no
pre-training, but it wasn't as hard to keep my eyes open
when I was looking up at him. It was strange seeing him
under those bright white lights. I'd got used to his face the
way it looked in the darkness, half covered in grime.

'Better late than never,' I said, my voice sounding like
I'd dragged my tongue over gravel. 'You look . . .'

He looked clean.

He looked pale.

He looked like he hadn't slept in months.

He had the same watery brightness in the whites of his
eyes that Mum had, and I knew she'd just left to cry.

He didn't look good.

Except the way he always looked good. Which still kind
of pissed me off.

'. . . alive.'

He laughed, and somehow looked even more tired for a
moment. 'Yeah. That's two of us. Thank God. Thank God,
that's two of us.'

JOE

She managed about an hour awake. Talking seemed like hard
work, so we spent the second half of it with her mum,

watching people try to sell off old tat they had in their attics.

Dad stopped by with Tesco sandwiches. I'd texted to tell him Peaches woke up, and he looked over at the bed, expectant. 'You going to introduce me, then?'

I knew he was wondering who this pale, wired-up, not-quite-dying girl I wouldn't leave alone was. I'd never mentioned her before. I'd never even known her.

I turned to the bed, wondering what Peaches was going to make of Dad and the spiderweb of tattoos that covered most of his skin. But she was sleeping again already, the bleeping of the machines by her side steady and even.

The next few days, she was awake more and more. Mum managed to get me to go home for a bit, while Tilda sat with her. I changed my clothes more often. Sometimes ate outside the hospital. But I didn't want to stay home. My phone was collecting a catalogue of missed calls and texts. People at school, or relatives I hadn't seen in a hundred years, were trying to get in touch. Journalists who'd managed to get my name off the internet somehow found my number.

Sam's sister. Doug's parents. They called too. I couldn't answer the phone to them yet, and I was terrified if I stayed at home too long I'd find them waiting at the door.

The hospital had started to feel more reassuring than anywhere else. It felt like inside those bright-painted walls was safer than out.

I had follow-ups on my knee. It was going to take a

while, but it didn't look like there was permanent damage. When I rang Dad he cheered down the phone.

Sometimes I'd bump into Violet in the halls or catch her getting coffee from one of the machines at a stupid time of night. She'd been in to see Peaches after she woke, and I'd stopped by her brother's room a couple of times. I didn't see Ellie. Violet said it wasn't touch and go any more exactly, but the longer it took her to wake, the less they knew about how she'd be when she did.

Neither of us wanted to leave the hospital.

'It's like if I look away for three seconds something could –'

'I know.' She smiled. I still don't know how she kept that smile.

Sometimes we'd just hold on to each other for a while by the vending machines, plastic cups of coffee getting more foul-tasting as they cooled in our hands. Then she'd go back to her brother, or Ellie, or to call her dad. And I'd find Peaches again.

PEACHES

He'd come skulking in in the middle of the night, trying not to wake me. The thing is, when all you have to do all day is sleep, you start to keep odd hours. When you're in hospital as long as I was, you kind of disassociate from the person in the bed. Your body's a thing that the nurses come in every couple of hours to prod at and check on, and to clip things to your fingers and ask you to give a number on a scale of one to ten. The rest of you is something separate. It floats. I spent a lot of time in a half-waking, half-sleeping state with my mind hovering just above the body in the bed, aware of but not really part of it.

And then Joe would come in and I'd be back. Human again, not just part of the general consciousness of the world. I suppose you'd say he kept me moored. That's what anchors do, isn't it?

Anyway, he'd come in, moving slowly, trying not to make a sound, and most of the time I'd be awake anyway.

'You don't have to tiptoe.'

I said it just to watch him start with surprise, blinking over to see me looking back.

'Sorry.'

'Don't you have a home to go to?' I asked.

Even Mum had started going home at nights. Visiting policies were supposed to be stricter, but we were the survivors of Hearne House and people trod around us as gently as Joe when he thought I was sleeping.

'Yeah, but the food's better here.' Dropping two Mars bars on to my tray table, he settled on the edge of my bed. Still looking knackered. I thought about offering him a swap. It would be a thrill to get to sit in a chair.

'Why are you awake?' he asked, before I could suggest he took the bed.

'Because the alternative is sleeping, and I've had enough of that to last me till Christmas. And, I don't know, I'm thinking.'

His expression flickered with worry. We both knew what being left alone with our thoughts meant.

'Not about that,' I said. 'Well, maybe parts of it.'

He kept his voice quiet, even though there was no one to disturb. 'Which parts?'

'Just the way we kept crossing over each other. You and me, Ellie and Violet and March. I know it's coincidence, but it feels important.'

'Does it?'

I tilted my chin up. 'Why are you still here, Joe?'

He shrugged one shoulder, leaning his hand down on the mattress beside me. 'I don't know. I guess you feel important, too.'

Letting out a breath, I looked away. Talking wasn't wearing me out any more, but I didn't have the right words.

Joe brushed the back of his hand against my cheek. 'You do.'

My eyes betrayed any attempt at disinterest, flicking back to meet his. I didn't want him to be here out of guilt, or because he felt sorry for me, or through some weird sense of responsibility, that was all. Nothing that had happened was his fault.

I tried a smile. It came out a little weak. 'You know, if this is you angling to kiss me again, now would be the time.

I'm sore and sweaty and bedridden. I believe I've reached the peak of my hotness.'

JOE

So I kissed her. Like I'd been thinking about kissing her, constantly, even while she'd been asleep. In some of my more desperate moments, early on when we still weren't completely sure she'd make it, I'd thought a kiss might be what would wake her.

I kissed her then. As gently as I could.

'Shit,' she whispered as I pulled back. Then: 'I wasn't trying to get you to. You didn't have to.'

I nodded. 'I know.'

'Oh.' She touched her fingertips to her lips as they curved into a soft, surprised smile. 'Well then, you don't have to do it again, either.'

She was right. I didn't.

So I did.

THIRTY-THREE

VIOLET

They told me that Ade was very lucky. It cannot be common to say that about a boy who has lost his mother. He was lucky that the bullets hit where they did, embedding themselves deep into bone but somehow missing the most vital parts. Lucky not to have been hit in places that would have bled out more readily. Lucky to be alive.

There is nothing about that which I can deny. I'd say that we are all lucky: Ade, my father and myself, to have been loved so very, very much.

She walked on after she was hit, they think. Further than should have been possible with such a wound. My mother. The bullet is most likely to have found her by the bridge, while I was further back, caught up in the crowds with Joe, frantic with her absence. She was found deep in the trees, wrapped over Ade so tightly that the police who cleared the grounds almost didn't realise he was there.

It was a long wait at the hospital that first night, before they matched the little boy they'd brought in with the girl being treated on a different ward, and came to tell me how lucky he was.

I wasn't alone. My father's sister called him when the news began to run unconfirmed stories of what was happening, and by the time I was carried into the hospital and sedated for shock there were aunties I'd never even met giving the reception desk my name. Claiming me as their blood even if I wasn't.

I couldn't save my father any pain when I told him. But he's stronger than I thought and I'm not alone in looking after him. I'm less alone than my mother ever was. There are so many people who want to help.

My mother never asked for help from anyone. Maybe she felt it would dent her pride. I know differently. It's not a bad thing to ask for – it's not wrong to not want to be alone. That there are so many people who care for my family enough to want to help is something I can only be proud of.

ELLIE

I dreamed about the explosion. You're not supposed to be able to dream in a coma. It's not a state like sleep, because sleep has cycles. It's a state of nothingness, a void where they put your brain so you can't feel anything.

But I dreamed. Perhaps that was just when I was close to waking up. In the dream I could see his blue eyes, as though some part of me was trying to recognise something in them. Humanity. I tried, but his stare was nothing but blue ice. Then the world caught fire. I was hit by a pressure wave that threw me back and down and doused me in unbearable heat. It wasn't painful, but the conscious part of me knew that it should be. After the white light faded into black again and the heat evaporated my face was still burning. Pressing a hand to my cheek to try and blot out the flames, I pulled my fingers back sticky.

I lay in the blackness and wondered how much of me remained.

VIOLET

I was allowed to see Ellie and my mother on the same day. Three days after Ambereve. Ade was on one of the wards, his condition considered stable. He hadn't cried. I think that everything was so strange and overwhelming he'd barely thought to. None of it was at all real.

It didn't feel real to me, pushing my father's chair down the aisle of the hospital chapel, where my mother's body had been laid out. My aunt stopped me to say that I didn't have to see her this way.

But I did. I had to see her, if it was going to be the last time.

It felt all wrong from the start, although what part could ever have felt right I don't know. Perhaps it was that she should have been at our own church, where she had taken me every Sunday and knew everyone. There should have been more people there, not just us three, moving as

313

slowly as we could towards the inevitable. There should have been song, joy and praise mixed with the sorrow.

But those were all things for later. This was just the first goodbye. I've learned since that when you lose someone you love, you have to say a thousand of them.

Our footsteps echoed.

She had been laid out in a coffin, low enough for my father to see her face without getting up from his chair. He cried out, a pain I recognised, and my aunt helped him place his hand where he could hold hers for a few final moments.

I studied her face and realised that, although I knew every detail of her, the most important parts of my mother weren't in that box. Her eyes were closed and her skin had tightened and taken an ashy tone that she would have tutted at in the mirror. Her cheeks seemed hollowed out. At her hairline a tiny part of the lace from her wig had started to peel. She would never have allowed herself to look less than put together.

Licking my finger, I smoothed the peeling spot back down.

Her skin was cold. It was cold when I kissed her cheek.

Wrong, I thought, shivering with a memory of the blankness I'd felt when I was looking for her that night. I'd never find her now, and that was wrong. It was wrong that when I took her hand she couldn't take mine back, her hands larger and stronger than mine, wrapping my fingers close.

It was wrong. It was wrong to have a world without

her. It was wrong that I was still living when the heart had been torn from my chest. It was wrong that I could hurt so much and not die from the pain. It was wrong that I could love someone so much and that love couldn't save them.

But in the wrongness I made her a promise. I promised that whatever I did in my life from now on, I would do it trying to be as happy as she'd always wanted me to be. I'd try to be as successful as she wanted, and as smart, and as put together, but I'd try to be happy most of all.

I didn't say those things to the woman laid in the box. I turned my eyes to the light in the chapel window. She is everywhere now. I know it. The most important parts of my mother are in me and in Ade and they're everywhere I look. I can just lift my eyes, even now, and know my words will reach her.

I promised her I would be happy. I promised I would not be alone.

When I went back to the hospital, I was told that Ellie's family had agreed to allow me to visit.

ELLIE

The burns covered most of my left cheek, stopping in an almost straight line at my nose – I must have turned my head. My clothes were melted into my skin down one side of my body: my arm and shoulder, hip and thigh and part of the way across my chest. I'd inhaled superheated air and burned my lungs from the inside out.

For just over two weeks, the induced coma kept me safe from knowing anything about it. I wasn't there for the first emergency surgeries, where they scraped off dead skin, managed swelling, replaced fluids. I missed my first few grafts, too: attempts to make the skin I had left fit across twice as much of me as it did before. When my parents tell me all the things I went through while I was unconscious, I can't fully understand how a human body can take so much and still function. I missed the worst of it, at least.

And I missed all Violet's first visits.

VIOLET

At first I was only able to come for a few minutes a day. There is a strict limit in the high-dependency burns ward: six patients to the ward and no more than two visitors at the bedside. Hours are limited and the possibility of infection means it's even more tightly controlled than the rest of the hospital.

But I went as often as I was able. The first time, Ellie was unrecognizable. The swelling made every part of her look impossibly tight. Part of her face was all but gone and the rest barely visible. A machine breathed for her, each inhale lifting her slightly off the bed. Alarms sounded, something to do with her body fighting the ventilation, and I left as nurses came to tend to her. They were so calm that it did a little to still the panicked whirlwind in my chest.

Ellie's mother caught my hand as I left, as though she knew. 'She's going to live through this,' she said, and I remembered what Ellie had told me. This wasn't the first time her mother had waited at the bedside of a child she could do nothing to help. 'She's a fighter, and everyone here's going to fight for her, so . . .' She trailed off. I watched her swallow against something in her throat. 'They told me they found you beside her.'

There were no words in me, only a small, painful sound. I nodded.

I hadn't known it would take someone else's mother hugging me as though she'd never let go before I could break down.

ELLIE

Waking up is a blur of dim aches and my parents' faces. I'd been taken off the ventilator before I'd been allowed to come round. Every breath was an effort but I was breathing for myself. I remember hearing scraps of information about pain relief, buttons I could press . . . things I wouldn't really know until I could move for myself. Mum remembers my first words on waking: 'What are all these people doing in my room?'

Violet came the day after, just for a few minutes. For some reason having her there made me nervous. I wasn't used

317

to being weak. 'I haven't asked for a mirror,' I told her. 'I know what it must look like.'

'You look beautiful,' she said.

VIOLET

She'd been in all the papers, of course. No one showed them to her, but in the bathrooms at the hospital I heard two women deep in discussion about the end of her perfect life.

I don't think that Ellie's life was ever perfect. Are any lives that way? But life itself is such a beautiful thing. The lift of Ellie's chest under her own breath was as stunning as she ever was in motion on the athletics track. Her being alive is the most beautiful thing to someone who almost felt her life slip between their fingertips.

She's beautiful in every way there is. I'll always think so.

ELLIE

I met Violet's brother after a month. I'd finally been moved to a non-intensive ward and they let me have the occasional visitor younger than twelve, although one of my favourite nurses still described children as 'walking disease vectors'.

He was so small, though I even felt small to myself. Healing burns wears out your muscles faster than anything else. Violet brought him in with her hands on his shoulders but I'd have recognised him easily. They both wore matching smiles.

We'd talked about what happened to her. All the people we'd lost. Her mother. Sam, who I'd known nearly as long as I'd known my own family. Who appears in my childhood photographs with that lopsided smile of his, chubby-cheeked and holding my hand. And Doug. Miss Ewell. My old athletics coach and two of the junior swimmers I trained with.

Joe came to sit with me sometimes too, and let me know how Peaches was doing, but he didn't want to talk about anyone who wasn't still here.

I kept the lists of names from the newspapers and read them often. Impossibly huge numbers of people we knew and people we didn't, but who belonged to us because of what we'd shared. I can't help feeling all those people are here with me today. Every day.

It meant so much to me to see Ade could still smile. He dragged his chair right up to the edge of the bed to say hello. 'Vi always talks about you.'

I raised my eyebrows. Eyebrow. 'She talks a lot about you, too.'

He rustled a comic out of his bag and spread it over my blankets. 'I brought you a story to read.'

Behind him, Violet clicked her tongue. 'It's his favourite.'

It was about ordinary people saving the world.

VIOLET

It was some time before March came to visit Ellie. He'd seen
Ade early on, and I'd run into him outside the burns ward
once, looking in through the glass at the six beds of the unit.
Six people so badly hurt that without this level of care they
wouldn't be alive.

I'd said he could come in. They allowed two visitors at
a time. But he waited until she was on the open ward and
well enough to talk.

I think he avoided spending too much time at the
hospital. His parents worked there and before long we all
knew who they were. A surgeon and consultant with tired,
kind eyes, trying to fix whoever they could, because their
daughter was beyond help now.

Hospital gossip and news reports were how I learned
that his sister had died.

'I don't like to hang around the hospital too much,' he
told Ellie, when he came to sit with us. 'People will think I'm
scared to be alone, and the last thing Imani would want me
to be is scared.'

ELLIE

'I'm scared,' I told him. 'I can't stop dreaming about it. I get
to sleep and suddenly it's all happening again.'

We'd studied wars at school. Saw distant things on
the news about attacks and bombings. Sometimes they

320

even came frighteningly close, but never so near that we hadn't felt untouchable.

I knew what a bomb sounded like, now. That still seemed impossible to me.

March bowed his head over the hands he kept steepled in his lap, as though he was at prayer. 'People who don't know my family well keep asking – kindly, most of them – if we ever expected to see this happen here. I'm Muslim, so somehow people think I've escaped from some part of the world where this sort of horror is routine. I'm from Morocco. I never saw violence while we lived there. My parents moved here only because they were offered good jobs.'

He went quiet, taking a breath as though there was something else to say, but no words big enough.

'You never thought you'd see it here either,' Violet said. March shook his head.

Violet sat down on the edge of the bed between us. 'I'm scared too. We've lived this now. It's not some distant horror that happened to other people. We can never pretend that we're *safe* again. This can never not be real, and that's frightening. But I'm more frightened that I'll allow fear to keep me from living. I'm going to live. Not being safe is all the more reason. I don't think we should allow those people to take away one more life.'

VIOLET

'I'm going to live, too,' March said. 'I'm far more afraid of how angry my sister would be with me if I didn't.'

He flashed a brief smile, then raised his eyebrows, plucking a comic book from the side of the bed. Ade must have left it there. 'Oh hey, my favourite.'

Ellie and I held hands for a long time after he'd gone.

I told her I was sorry about the nightmares, and she shrugged the shoulder not bandaged down. 'They're in a part of my brain I can't control. When I'm awake it's easier. I go back there when I'm sleeping, but waking up every day feels like a reminder that I was lucky enough to get out.'

We both were. They call us that in the newspapers now, when they run updates to say how our lives are going on. We are the survivors. The lucky ones.

THIRTY-FOUR

MARCH

Since we moved to England I've been two people. Majid at home with my family, and at school, March.

It was an accident, becoming this second me. The teacher who introduced me to my first British classroom trailed off halfway through the word 'Majid' as though she was afraid of it. 'Please welcome Maj . . .'

And the class turned something foreign into something familiar. Maj became March. I hated it then, but in those days I spoke Darija, and better French than I did English, so I'd quickly learned to keep quiet.

Now everyone at school knows my name. I've gone back, of course. I don't intend to give some terrorists my exam results, too. There are a small band of us there, the ones who were at Hearne House until the end. Some of us stick together, while for the others it's the last thing they want to be associated with. Whichever option we picked, nobody would hesitate over our names any more.

I can be Majid wherever I choose. Good. I want my true name to be known.

But I've begun to like March. I think I'll keep it, too.

It's the moment before spring, the time when things start
to change for the better. And an instruction to keep
moving, always.

ELLIE

I got home for Christmas. For a few days, at least. That's
how the recovery process is working out right now. A
weekend at home followed by more time in hospital or in the
rehab unit. I've been told to expect to be getting surgeries for
a couple more years – the doctors are working to fill in the
smudged parts of who I used to be, like artists restoring a
painting. I see the physio twice a week to rebuild some
strength, because healing from burns also burns right through
your muscle. And I go to the counselling sessions, even when
I don't want to.

I don't know if I'll run again, or swim, or cycle. I won't
be Ellie Kimber the triple threat any more. But I want to
make clear it's not because of my injuries. If that life had ever
been something I wanted for myself, I'd fight to get back
there, but I've thought about it and that's not the thing I
want to fight for.

If I run again, it will just be for me. I think I might like
that. I never really ran for myself before.

The thing I really want to go back to is the modelling.
I could be quietly grateful that the worst of my injuries are
on my deaf side, turn my face away and let myself not hear

what people say when they see me. But I don't intend to allow that. Seeing my face in magazines the way it looks now feels more important than it ever did before. It might sound impossible, after all this, but if the experience taught me anything it's that there are no impossible things.

PEACHES

I'm not officially a drop-out yet, but I'm working on it. Mum suddenly developed enough passionate interest in my education to convince me to take my GCSEs, and after that I'm leaving to do something I care about. There's a young directors' scheme at a theatre in the city I'm going to apply for. I figure it's time to come down from the gantries and let myself be seen, even if it's only as a shadowy figure giving notes from a dark auditorium.

Moz used to talk about starting a theatre company. He said we had better ideas than any of them. I'll name mine after him one day.

JOE

I've been sort of stuck.

PEACHES

Right now, though, I'm treading water. I haven't felt ready for school yet. I'm not-really-studying for the exams I promised to take.

I'm spending a lot of time with Joe. He helps. I like to think we help each other a little.

JOE

It feels hard to get back into things. Like the whole world completely changed and people keep acting as though nothing's wrong. There are gaps everywhere – holes in the world – and if you're not watching where you're going, you might not notice them until you've fallen in.

Like when I went back to Clifton.

Everyone said it would help. School. Give me something else to think about. Dad even walked me there, which was embarrassing as hell, and left me at the gates like a five-year-old.

I got up to the wall by the dining hall. That's where whichever of the three of us got in first would wait, because we all came from different directions. Sam's house was on an estate just out of town and Doug got the bus.

I could see Doug scuffing the trainers his mum kept cleaning for him up against the brick dust. Sam arranging chewed gum to spell out something obscene. One of them yelled over at me, 'You're late, mate. Did baby need a lie-in?'

The wall was empty.

And things just sort of blacked out there, except for this tightness in my chest that was making it hard to breathe. Felt like I think a heart attack must do, and it would be typical to go out to one of those, wouldn't it? After everything.

It was panic. A panic attack.

They literally called an ambulance for my panic and the paramedic explained that it can feel like death but it's just your mind convincing your body to react more dramatically than it needs to. I've had a few since. It's like my brain keeps throwing 'what if's at me, and I don't have any answers.

I haven't tried going back to school again yet. I'm thinking about transferring, somewhere there are fewer gaps and empty, familiar places.

PEACHES

We go for walks when we should be in lessons. Pick a direction and just go. It's kind of incredible how much of our own town we'd never noticed before. There are hidden parks, places where you turn the corner and the houses open out into a square of green, and odd little shops on roads so quiet it makes you wonder how they ever do business.

It's calming. Knowing there's all that space around me makes it easier to breathe.

And I've even spent some time at the running track. *Not* my natural habitat.

JOE

So instead of school, I'm training. Dad drops me off at the track even though I can tell he's sick of the early mornings already, and sometimes we pick Peaches up on the way. She doesn't sleep that well. Neither of us do. But having her there keeps the panic from settling in whenever the place feels too crowded or too empty. I just find where she's sitting on the sides and it's OK.

It's OK.

VIOLET

My aunt – the one I have related by blood as well as love – is moving in with us as soon as my father is well enough to come home. There was a thought that we might move to her, but our house is larger and not so far away that she can't travel for work. My cousins are all grown and moved.

She tells me often that she can't replace my mother but she has a mother's love to spare.

For now my studies are part-time, but I'm looking forward to going back to school. Seeing the friends I have there. Working. Life is strange without a routine, so I've kept to one I've created for myself. I take Ade to his school in the morning and in the afternoon I see Ellie. We get coffee at the hospital, or on days when she's at home we sit in her lounge watching the kind of movies my mother wouldn't have allowed in ours.

Ellie still needs so much care, but she won't let me be involved with that. She tells me, 'I want to be the one thing in your life you're not trying to look after.' I think that it helps her, too, to have someone who won't flinch or fuss over her. We are each other's respite.

I see the others often. March, and Joe and Peaches. Peaches is often at the hospital, with Joe rarely far behind her. For all we should know now that safety is an illusion, it always feels safer together.

PEACHES

March started the group. It's not supposed to be counselling, or to replace it. It's not supposed to be anything, really. Half the time we just hang out and play computer games: car racing or fantasy stuff where you feed dragons and weave baskets. None of us are up for shoot-outs any more.

When it started, we'd meet at Ellie's bedside (special pity-dispensation for more than two visitors: we nearly died and we're not afraid to use it). We'd just read comics or talk about TV. Now he texts us the location: the hospital coffee shop and the Kimbers' front room get the most use.

Meeting of the Lucky Ones. You free?

MARCH

Other people kept calling us that, and I know how it feels to be given a new name you never asked for. You can either hate it or you can own it.

We've all been asked the same questions over and over by people who weren't there and won't ever understand what it was like, even if they read these transcripts. Even if we all talked about it for another week. But the questions I get asked are sometimes different from the rest.

'I suppose you're used to it?'

No, as I've said.

'You must be glad the killers weren't Muslim.'

I understand why they ask this, ignorant as it is. Terror and hate have a long history through every colour, race and creed. It's something humans are capable of, but only a strange and abhorrent few. Thankfully, only a few.

So, no, I'm not glad that the terrorists weren't of my religion. I think it's a shame they were of my species.

And one last question, the one we all get over and over, because nobody who didn't live through it can understand.

'You must feel so lucky?'

ELLIE

It's not a new nickname, for me. They told me I was lucky to outlive my brother, while my parents alternated between making sure I felt loved and finding it hard to look at me in their grief.

If survival is all that luck means, then I'm one of the lucky ones.

JOE

I finally spoke to Sam's and Doug's parents at the funeral. They had one ceremony for both of them. There were so many funerals for a few weeks after that it made sense.

All the photos had us three looking out of them, like we were part of a human chain. Doug, Sam and Joe. Joe, Doug and Sam. You could call one of us and two others would look round. So it was right to see their coffins next to each other. We'd been together for years.

They just went and died without me.

The service was like watching the fuzz on a TV screen when the signal's broken. Jumbled-up fragments, impossible to make sense of. I didn't cry until I walked outside afterwards and Doug's mum was the first person I saw. I guess she'd gone out for a bit, to breathe.

She's a baker, Doug's mum. When we were kids she used to let us make bread rolls with her, carving our initials into the top so she'd be able to tell afterwards which ones weren't fit for human consumption. S, D, J.

Always the three of us.

Peaches was still in hospital and I'd slipped free from

my parents. I was alone with her and just crying and saying sorry, over and over. I'm sorry I lived and they didn't. I'm sorry I was the one. I'm sorry, I'm sorry.

Sometimes I still feel like that even now. Sometimes living feels like the unluckiest thing of all.

But sometimes it doesn't. When I think about all the things I don't want to miss. Blue skies and cold mornings and my sisters' graduations, and Dad watching me run, and Mum and Ellie and March and Violet. And Peaches.

It's taking me a while to get my life back on track, but I'm going to. I want to live. If that's luck, then I'm not going to waste it.

PEACHES

Am I lucky? Every night they light the bonfire. Every night I sit high on the gantry with Moz, watching the torches follow the trail up the hill, knowing what they're walking into. And I still can't stop it. It doesn't stop.

JOE

Sometimes I close my eyes and see Sam and Doug dying all over again. Sometimes I close them and we're all watching Ellie Kimber dance.

ELLIE

I used to think there was no such thing as too loud. My parents stood way back from the main stage that night because of the noise. 'TOO LOUD,' Dad had mouthed just before I'd broken away to run towards the speakers. 'TOO LOUD.' I wanted to surround myself in the music. Couldn't understand how anything, *anything* could be loud enough to satisfy me.

Now I know. When a car backfires, or someone drops something with an unexpected bang, I understand how there can be a too loud.

I carry that night with me in ways I'm still finding out about. I always will. But I carry other things with me too, closer to my heart.

VIOLET

There are days when grief still takes me by surprise. I drop Ade off at school. I visit Ellie, I take the bus home and, when I am alone, I sob as I think of my mother's hands in my hair.

I've taken my braids out. No one will ever do them with her care.

But I feel braver than I used to. My mother isn't with me, but I talk to her everywhere and I tell her the future I'll have. When I think of her, I think that she would be surprised by me, but also proud. Sometimes I feel her hand on my shoulder. It is guiding me, but it isn't holding me back.

I am lucky to have had such love, and lucky for the love I have now.

PEACHES

I don't sleep well, but the hours I'm awake are brighter than they've ever been. We all lost things in the attack. I think I gained things, too. It wasn't a fair trade – not one I'd have asked for. But this is the life I have now. It's a life I could have lost three times.

I'm going to use it.

JOE

And when we all get together, at March's meetings, it's like some of the empty spaces in the world close up. I can start to let myself think that there might be a day when remembering Doug and Sam won't feel so raw – so much like something that's been sliced out of my skin. I can almost believe that missing them will turn into feeling glad they were there.

I've never been good at being alone. But I'm not. I can reach out, any time, and Violet's answering the phone sleepily, because I've forgotten that she thinks nine p.m.'s a reasonable time for bed. Or Ellie's asking for distractions from the boredom of another hospital stint. March is letting me know he's beaten my score on *Mario Kart*.

And there's Peaches. She's my constant. Texting me

can't sleep with flawless timing on nights when I've just woken from the worst of my dreams. Climbing into Dad's car in the arse-crack of the morning, bleary-eyed and telling me the worst thing about my athletic ambitions is that they clash with the hours McDonald's serve breakfast. Playing me all her favourite musicals and telling me the *next one* is going to make me fall in love.

And usually she's right.

But it's always with her.

MARCH

Sometimes the papers run stories about what they're planning to do with Hearne House now. There's talk of knocking it down or building it up into a monument to the ones who died. Whichever they decide, it doesn't bother me. That place doesn't bother me at all. The dead aren't there any more, and their murderers don't own its legacy. Death doesn't stalk across the bridge over the river or roam the corridors of the house, so I'm not afraid of it.

When I look back on that night, I remember people making space for others to hide, even if it meant they might be seen themselves. I remember mothers cradling their children to keep them from harm. Friends arm in arm as they walked away or holding hands as they died.

I remember love, despite everything.

If anything remains in that place, it can only be love.

AUTHOR'S NOTE

I can't remember a time in my life when terrorism hasn't
influenced my world. Although the Good Friday agreement
was signed in 1998, putting an end to most terror attacks
linked to the Northern Ireland conflict, I grew up in
Guildford, just down the street from one of two pubs that
had been blown up by terrorists before I was born. My
parents had been living in a flat right across the road when
the bomb went off. They'd felt the ground shake under their
feet, and had seen the wreckage. My dad also worked at
Harrods, the scene of another bombing where six people
were killed.

London when I was little was still a city of temporary
Tube closures and suspect packages, of museum evacuations
during school trips, and people telling you not to stand too
close to the glass. I have very early memories of waiting up
for my parents to come home from work, but not being
entirely sure that they would.

Now, again, it often seems like terrorists make the news
every week, somewhere in the world. The senseless, showy
violence can feel very frightening and very close. But there
are a few things it's important to remember about terrorism.

Mainly that it doesn't work, and terrorists never win. It's been studied and statistically proven (for example, in a book by Audrey Kurth Cronin titled *How Terrorism Ends*) that not one extremist group since the 1970s has succeeded in obtaining its goals by carrying out terror attacks. It would seem that the opposite is true: in trying to scare us, they make us more determined to stand up and stand stronger against them.

Although the events you hear about on the news – like the fictional attack described in this book – claim lives and have a lasting impact on many more survivors, which must never be underestimated, most terrorist attacks are not calculated and deadly. Many of them fail spectacularly. Underwear bomber Umar Farouk Abdulmutallab tried to become a suicide bomber, but only managed to burn his own bits. In 2007, terrorists attacked Glasgow airport, only to be dragged out of the car they were trying to use as a weapon and beaten up by unimpressed Scots.

Terrorism feels like a constant in our world but, as March says, it has a long past and can't be attributed to one group of people. The terrorists of my childhood were white men. Many of the terrorists of my present still are. The resilience, hope and humour shown by the survivors of the attack on Utoya island by Anders Breivik was one of many dozens of influences on this book. So too were the survivors of attacks in Paris, Orlando, Boston, Nice, Istanbul, Tunisia, New Delhi, Mumbai, Bali, Baghdad and many more places where terror has shaken the ground out from under people. *This Can Never Not Be Real* was written before the Manchester Arena Bombing in 2017, but I can't overlook the bravery and resilience of the survivors of that atrocity, and the love and support the city showed in its wake. Freya Lewis, who survived the attack, told her story in her book *What Makes Us Stronger*. In times of terror, I always want to hear about the people who survive. We are flooded with pictures of the terrorists, and hear their causes analysed and criticised, but I'm with Violet – it doesn't matter what reasons these people think they have. There is *no* reason good enough to commit an act of terror. The attackers deserve much less attention. I want to hear about those who were lost too soon, and even more than that – those who live. It's their names I want to know.

As such, the terrorists' actions are part of this book, but I have left the terrorists themselves and their specific motivation out of the picture. Suffice to say that there are people of many different beliefs and persuasions who labour under the misapprehension that violence is the way to get their voice heard. If we are ever to see an end to this, we must show them that it is not. Drown killers in silence and amplify survivors' words.

I've tried to be careful not to glorify any of the violence, while not hiding it from view. This is a story told in the survivors' voices, and it's not their responsibility to explain why this happened. They survived, and they will go on surviving every day for the rest of their lives. That's enough.

The characters in this book are forced into the realization that sudden, inexplicably terrible things can happen in any place, at any time. They don't stop for weekends, or holidays, or even for pandemics. There is no way for most of us to make sense of, or predict, these events. And I know the thought of that can be scary. But it's precisely because life itself is so entirely unpredictable that there's no point in letting fear control us. We can't protect ourselves by stopping living – by not going to that party, or festival, or on that train. The way to oppose terrorism is to live the best lives we can, and love as many people as possible. I wish that for us all.

'What will survive of us is love.'
Philip Larkin, *An Arundel Tomb*

ACKNOWLEDGEMENTS

I wrote this book before the Covid-19 pandemic gave the whole world an object lesson in loss and survival. I wrote it while a series of losses, including my Mum, was giving the same directly to me. These are lessons I don't think we ever stop learning: loss is always unbearable, survival often feels impossible, but it's so much better if we don't have to do it alone. So I have to start by thanking, if not for the first time, some of the people whose friendship and support helped me through: Jo, Talia, Katy, Gee, Ruxi, Hannah, Lindsey, Ashley, Mici. Erica, and everyone at work. Maria, I hope you know you've been a lifesaver more than once.

And Dad. I hope we've helped each other. Love you.

Getting a book like this together is no mean feat, especially during a pandemic. It's the book of my heart and I'm eternally grateful for the people who saw so clearly all that it meant and who have taken it into their hearts, too. Ali Dougal, I'll always be so glad this book found its way to you.

Then there's everyone at Farshore who have been a delight from the very first moment, and nothing but warm, gorgeous and supportive throughout this strange year. Especially my editor, Sarah Levison. I feel so lucky to be working with you. To the whole team: Lindsey Heaven and Lucy Courtenay, Laura Bird, Jennie Roman, Aleena Hasan, Olivia Carson, Jasveen Bansal, Siobhan McDermott, Leah Woods and Ingrid Gilmore, you're all wonder workers and dream makers, thank you.

There is no one I'd rather go into the publishing trenches with than my agent, Molly Ker Hawn. Thanks also to Amelia Hodgson, Victoria Capello and the crack team at The Bent Agency for all the help this year.

There are a few readers, bloggers and bookish types who may not know how much they've brightened my days – thanks to Amy-Jane, Michele, Demet, Kirsten, James and more.

And to the people who helped me with the book right from the start: friends, other writers, early readers, diversity and inclusivity readers, and people who helped with the technical bits that didn't all make it into the story but still informed it: Cordelia Lamble, who read this book in small chunks as I wrote it, and whose every exclamation mark kept me writing. Kathryn Clarke, Sarah House, Ros Stimpson, Julie Pike, C.J. Skuse, Shireen Naaz, Laura Steven, Sophie Cameron, Josh, Stef, Habiba, Roger and Andrew. You're all excellent, thank you.

Elliot (Ellie), thank you for the loan of your name. This book is for my mum. They all are.

Look out for Sera Milano's
next book for young adults

. . . .

COMING SOON